# DON'T BLINK

## —AN URBAN NOVEL—

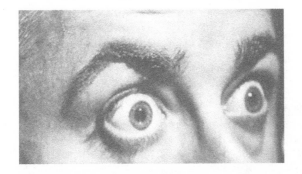

Curtis Jones

M000102674

Copyright © 2019 Curtis Jones
All rights reserved
First Edition

PAGE PUBLISHING, INC.
New York, NY

First originally published by Page Publishing, Inc. 2019

ISBN 978-1-64424-421-0 (Paperback)
ISBN 978-1-64424-419-7 (Digital)

Printed in the United States of America

To all my family and friends who supported me
during this journey, thanks beyond words. Your
belief and encouragement made this possible.

# A HUSTLER'S CREED

Days without ending, alone with your thoughts
Bars all around you. The price that crime brought
Shackles and handcuffs, name on your chest
Food that they give you, fit for roaches at best
Pride stripped away, your dignity bare
Abuse to be taken, strike back if you dare
Shame to be taken, you don't have a voice
Time to lock in, they give you no choice
If you're a good boy, you'll be out in about ten
But living this way makes beasts out of men
Day finally comes, you've earned your release
Can't get a job, you're a con in the streets
So what do you do, you've nowhere to run
Go back to your old way, the way of the gun
A shot goes off loud for all to hear
Now maybe the warden won't turn a deaf ear
'cause even though now, you're back in a cell
You've just sent his loved one to heaven or hell

# CHAPTER 1

The tall man moved with the stealth of a jungle cat as he flittered from shadow to shadow, seemingly becoming invisible as he crept from block to block until he came to the high-rise project unit he sought. He melted into the darkness, crossing the street to another high-rise that was abandoned but facing the unit he was seeking. He quickly ascended the rickety stairs, comparing lines of sight to the fifth-floor window in which the man he had come to kill lived. The 7.62 Mannlicher rifle that came with a nighttime scope that turned the surrounding darkness into daylight and easily fit into the briefcase was in his left hand. Assembly was a snap, and three minutes later, he nestled down into his sniper's lair, barrel resting securely on the rooftop edge. As he peered through the scope, the party going on in room 517 appeared to be in full swing as his target and five of his henchmen drank Henny, smoked weed, and watched the three highly paid strippers performed dance moves that defied gravity. Suddenly, his target stood up and pulled a thick wad of cash from his pocket and proceeded to make it rain on the big booty chick who was bouncing in a split, making her ass cheeks clap like thunder. The sniper drew in a deep breath, held it, and sighted on his target's left ear. A quiet *pffft* escaped the barrel of the silenced rifle, and a split second later he saw his target topple to the right, minus the left side of his head. He could hear the screams of the strippers and the confused shouts of the stunned henchmen as they saw their leader's brains and gore run down the wall. They all snatched up their guns and ran outside, seeking revenge and retaliation, but the sniper had long since disappeared back into the shadows he had so quietly and efficiently appeared from.

# CHAPTER 2

Blink turned the corner on 125th and Brodner Street in his custom-made Beemer, the sounds of Usher's "Confessions" banging from the twelve-inch woofers he had specially mounted in his trunk. He knew that all eyes were on him, but his mind was a thousand miles away as he contemplated the problems he faced. Ever since Snowman got his brains blew out last week, the product had been hard to come by, and Blink had to find another connect soon or he risked losing the clientele it had taken so long for him to build up. The problem was that the dope he had access to now had been stepped on so many times the dope fiends were complaining and beginning to take their business to the other side of town. As he pulled over to the curb in front of the all-day diner, he spotted his LT and right-hand man, Big Jeff, coming out with a chicken box in his hand, licking his fingers.

"Boy, that greasy food is gonna kill you one day for sure," he shouted as he slid from his ride to dap his man up.

"Better this food than one of these fool ass niggers," Jeff replied as he returned the love.

"We've got to get on something like yesterday," Blink said. "Things are getting tight with what we're holding, and niggers are sho nuff starting to bitch and moan."

"Yeah, I know what you mean," Jeff replied. "Our runners tell me that they only have enough product left until this evening, and our money has been short because they have to take shorts."

"I know, but I have one last card I'm about to play to see if I can turn this shit around," Blink said. "Come on and ride with me." Jeff hopped into the passenger seat just as Blink said, "Don't get no grease on my interior. I just had this motherfucker detailed." Blink wasn't a major playa. He only pushed around four keys a week, and his crew was small compared to some of the dealers who were on that bump and grind in a monster way.

He always told himself that he was only in this for the short term, just long enough to purchase the auto repair and accessories shop that has been his dream to own. He figured that, at the rate he was going, in less than a year, he would be able to realize his goal. His plan was to provide jobs for his people that would provide a legitimate income and not contribute to the urban decay that was so much a part of his daily life. But for right now, "A nigga gotta do what a nigga gotta do" was his motto because the banks just didn't give business loans to people like him. Right now, he only hoped that the phone call he received last night was righteous and that the promise of a new connect proved fruitful.

As he blended into the traffic heading south on I 95, he glanced over at his partner, Big Jeff, who was bobbing his head to the beat without a care in the world. They had met in elementary school after Blink stood beside him, fighting off the local toughs who tried to take Jeff's lunch money. Blink admired the boy's nuts as he stood up for himself and battled tooth and nail. In return, Jeff never forgot Blink having his back, and he had been loyal to Blink ever since. "Look, homey, this is my first time doing business with these niggas, so stay sharp and keep a close eye on how things go down."

"That's word" Blink replied "Boy, I got your back, and if things look funky, you best believe my ratchet gonna clap," Jeff said. "We been down for each other too long to let shit get out of hand now. What's word, but these DC niggas got a different way of doing shit. But this nigga Nut seems like he's the one. We'll know in a minute."

That being said, Blink reached over and turned up the volume as DMX came on to tell you what a dog likes. Blink pulled into a gas station on Rhode Island Avenue and hit Nut up from one of the few remaining pay phones in the area. After three rings, Nut answered, "Hey, what's up, partner? You touched down on this end yet?"

"Yeah, we bout three blocks away from where you said you wanna meet, so we should be there in about five minutes."

"Cool," Nut replied. "I'll be in the black Denali. See you then."

Blink pulled up at the McDonald's parking lot four minutes later and slid next to the Denali that was already there. He slid out of the seat as Nut did the same, and the two men exchanged hugs and greetings as this was their first face-to-face meeting since each left the penitentiary where they met. A mutual respect that developed behind the walls evolved into a friendship that lasted outside of them. "My man," Nut spoke. "Good to see you on this side of the fence. Ready to get this money?"

"Hell yeah," said Blink. "Let's both get paid."

"I've got ten keys of pure I'll let you have at $15,000 each. You can step on it four times, and it'll still be the best in the city."

"Damn," Blink responded. "I only came strapped to purchase four. I wish I had known."

"You know you my guy, so I'll give you the others on consignment," said Nut. "I know you're good for it."

"Now that's love," gushed Blink.

"Give me a week and I'll have that for you."

"No doubt, partner," said Nut. "Hey yo," he screamed to one of his goons. "Take Blink's man to the spot and hit him off with ten of those things."

"We'll be here waiting for you."

Blink and Nut went inside and rehashed old times as Blink slipped him the $60,000 he had on him. After twenty minutes, Jeff pulled back up in the parking lot looking like he hit the lottery. After exchanging hugs again Blink pulled back out to head home, knowing that he had surely stepped his game up.

# CHAPTER 3

The sniper sat in the living room of his modest three-bedroom house in the county, surrounded by photos of his loved ones and memories of happier times. His eyes as well as his mind were constantly drawn back to the picture of his only daughter, a vision of loveliness and joy captured during the night of her senior prom. She looked so much like her mother that his heart ached, and he couldn't prevent the tear that escaped his eye from rolling down his cheek. Silently he uncoiled his six-by-six-inch frame from the couch to grasp the picture in his large hands, gazing at it intently as if that very act would bring her back to him.

Suddenly, a fit of rage possessed his core, and he sat the picture back on the mantelpiece with shaking hands. "I promise you, Denise, I promise you that before I am through, they will all pay for what they did to you. For what they did to my family. They will be sorry."

He headed down to his finished basement, clicked on the light, and surveyed the instruments of death he had arrayed according to their firepower. Everything from an assassin's 22 Beretta to a shoulder-held missile launcher lay before him, and he selected a .45 caliber Smith and Wesson and powerful Radon night vision field glasses. Tonight's mission was more about reconnaissance than engagement. He pulled the list from his shirt pocket that had fifteen names on it. The first five were crossed out, the last being that of Bernard "Snowman" Jackson. Everyone crossed out had already met bloody and violent ends, and everyone on that list had one common denominator—all were drug dealers. He memorized the address of number 6, put the sheet of paper in his wall safe, and melted out into the night.

Blink sat on the steps of the high-rise where two of his stash houses were, watching the action of the night unfold. He kept a close eye on his runners—not because he did not trust them, but the streets had been talking, and supposedly, there was a loose cannon going around who had declared war on dealers. Whether or not this extended to street-level runners or just upper management had yet to be determined, but he never took chances with the lives of those within his circle. This was the one characteristic that made him different from other players while serving to endear him to those in the hood and those who used his product.

"Yo, Jeff, how we looking tonight?" Jeff came up off the hood of the Yukon he had been leaning on, trying to rap up this pretty young thing that had cruised by here earlier. Looking good Cowboy, its hand over fist out here.

"The fiends are raving about our shit and keep coming back for more. I'm gonna have to bust out and go grab a re-up for the runners in bout an hour."

"That's music to my ears B, 'cause I'm gonna hit up Nut to let him know we'll be down there this weekend to touch him with the rest of that cash. While we're at it, we might as well see how many more bucks we can grab," replied Blink.

"What honey in the Kon talking bout?"

"She wants to hook up later tonight at Club Shake Off, trying to see if you want to hang because she has the real homegirl for you."

"Naw, Jack, I'mma have to pass tonight. Got to run over to the east side and holler at mom's. I haven't seen her in a minute and you know she's been blowing my phone up. Tell honey I'll have to take a rain check."

Blink hopped in his Lex and put in R. Kelly's new CD as he took the scenic route crosstown. His mother, Mrs. Kathy, lived in the same house Blink has been born in twenty-three years earlier. She was a lovely, statuesque woman and had passed her good looks down to her only son. Blink stood 6 feet 2 inches and 190 pounds with the wavy hair and high cheekbones that bespoke of his African-American and Native American mixture. His even pearly white teeth, dimples, and copper-colored eyes set many females panties on fire, and even though he knew it, it wasn't a big deal to him. "Looks fade, money doesn't" was his motto, and he was determined not to let anything impede on his paper chase.

As he turned down the tree-lined street his mom lived on, he noticed a late-model Ford pulling away from the curb in front of his mother's house, and it seemed as if the driver was making sure his face was not seen. He averted his head, refusing to meet Blink's inquiring gaze, and sped up as the two cars passed each other. Blink shrugged his shoulders and pulled up in his mother's driveway, giving his horn a short blast to announce his arrival. Bounding through the front door his nostrils were instantly greeted by the smell of his favorite meal—fried chicken, corn on the cob, mashed potatoes, and sweet tea. Nobody cooked fried chicken like his mother, not Popeye's, Colonel Sanders, or Gino's. His mother already was standing by the kitchen sink washing the dishes and placing them on the drying rack as he grabbed her by the waist and planted a big wet kiss on her cheek.

"Hey, dear lady, how's it going?" he asked as she shoved him away with one hand.

"Go on now. You're gonna mess up my hair, and you know I have a Bible meeting to go to this afternoon," Mrs. Cathy said, all the while reveling in her son's attention. "Go wash up while I make you a plate." Blink went upstairs to the bathroom that seemed to get smaller with age. Many times, he'd tried to get her to move to a condo or apartment where she'd have an easier time of it, but each time she'd refused. "Too many memories in these four walls," she'd exclaim. Blink's daddy had passed away in the upstairs bedroom from a bout with colon cancer when Blink was fifteen. His dad had refused to expire in the hospital, insisting that they take him home so he could be with his loved ones as he passed from this world to the next. And though he was a serious hustler in the late '70s to early '80s, he didn't leave much behind except the house and the 1988 Oldsmobile in the driveway. However, Cathy cherished his memory and refused to leave the past behind.

"Howard, hurry up and come downstairs. Your plate is getting cold," shouted his mom. She was the only person he knew that used his government name, having been called Blink since early childhood because of an affliction that caused rapid eye movement. Surgery had taken care of that, but the nickname stuck. Blink came down and ate like there was no tomorrow as his mother hovered in the background, ready to wait on him if there was anything else that was needed. She was extremely proud of her boy, and being a hustlers' wife, she knew the game he was involved in; and while not condoning it, she long ago decided that what would be would be.

"Honey, I hope you being careful out there in those streets. You know it's not like it was when your father was out there anymore. You have to worry about those around you as well as the police nowadays. It's just so hard to trust anyone."

"Don't worry, Mom. I got this," Blink said. "You know I don't let anyone but Jeff know my business. He's like my right arm."

"Okay, sweetie. You just be careful. I don't know what I would do if something were to happen to you."

Blink stood up and placed his dishes in the sink. "Now you just go on and have yourself a good time at Bible study tonight. As long as I got you praying for me, nothing can't happen to me 'cause I know you got a direct line to the man upstairs."

Ms. Cathy threw a playful swing that Blink easily evaded and went upstairs. Blink removed an envelope containing five crisp hundred-dollar bills that he placed on the dining room table where his mother was sure to see it. He hollered upstairs, "Bye, Mom. See you soon" and was out the door. Since he had no immediate issues to take care, of, he picked up his cell and dialed Kimmy, his on-again-off-again girlfriend. She picked up on the first ring.

"Oh, so you finally got around to dialing my number, huh? You must either be bored or horny because those are the only times I hear from you."

"See, there you go again," Blink shot back. "I can't even get a kind greeting out of you and the only reason I called was because you were on my mind."

"Uh-huh, so you say," said Kimmy, already starting to ease up.

"Where you at and what you doing? I'm just leaving my mom's and on my way to you," replied Blink. "How 'bout we take in a movie and a couple of drinks?"

"I don't feel like going to no loud-ass club. Why don't you let me think about it while I take a shower and I'll see you when you get here?"

"Sounds good to me," said Blink, peeling away from the curb with visions of Kimmy's luscious young body dancing in his head.

The sniper pulled up down the block from Blink's main stash house, watching the transactions as a fiend would slide up, palm a bill into one dude's hand, and be directed to the lobby of the project building to be served by another runner. It was all done smoothly, and if the police were to grab the moneyman, he would have no dope on him and claim harassment. If they tried to run a raid in the stash house, the lookouts on the rooftops would spot them coming from a long way off and signal the moneyman with a flashlight, who, in turn, would signal the doorman in the house, and the dope in the house would be moved through the back to an entirely different location till the heat died down. So far it had been foolproof, and Blink had never taken a hit, but then again, he had never had this much product to move. In his absence, Jeff made sure everything moved like clockwork, but he was totally unaware of the sniper's presence. The sniper knew Jeff wasn't the main man. In fact, he chided himself on almost being spotted and recognized by Blink as he cased his mother's house. He was forced to do so because he was yet to find out where Blink laid his head and only had his mother's address to go on. He frowned as he recalled the curiosity etched on Blink's face as he drove past; he had lingered too long in front of the house in the belief that Blink was out handling his business. He shrugged as there was little he could do about it now, just had to make sure that the next time he and Blink crossed paths would be the last.

He checked his watch and saw that Jeff made sure to shut it down at exactly 11:00 p.m. as they did every night and watched him slide into his silver-and-black Audi 9000. The sniper decided to follow Jeff to see where this would lead because he was determined that not only was Blink and his crew doomed, so was the supplier who had put the drugs into Blink's hands as well. He slipped his car into gear and followed at a discreet distance.

Jeff had already made plans to meet up with the honey he had met earlier on the strip at the club, but first he wanted to go home to take a shower and get fresh. He had also told part of the crew that he would pick them up to hang out, so he was in a hurry and took no notice of the car shadowing his every move. As he pulled up to the apartment he shared with his cousin Tony, he wondered if he had time to cop a bag of that 'dro that his homeboy Drake was bumping. Never knowing that he was being scrutinized, he ran on in the front door, deciding to cop on the way out. All he had in mind was the way Shorty was licking that lollipop and the sexy look she had in her eyes.

The sniper decided to wait on Jeff, and after about twenty-five minutes, he was rewarded with the sight of him coming back downstairs decked out in his Butter Tims, fitted retro Lakers jersey, and black jeans. His Lakers hat was sat at a cocky angle, and he had on two chains that bumped against his chest as he ran, catching the reflection off every light and looking like they had cost a grip. After deciding that Jeff was probably just out for a night of debauchery, the sniper headed home for some much-needed rest; he had been up for the better part of the day and night. The time for retribution was nearing, and he had to be at his best to make sure it was delivered.

Jeff and his soldiers Byrd, Moon, Lil Harve, and Shiny bounced up to the entrance of the club looking like a rap group. All of them felt underdressed because, usually, wherever they went, they all were strapped, but they had to leave their burners this time. No way were they gonna pass the security at the front door packing, especially since the majority of the bouncers were moonlighting NYPD officers. As they entered to the extra loud bass, thumping from one of Tupac's classics, Byrd shouted, "Man, ain't nothing but wall-to-wall pussy up in here tonight. I know I'm going home with something." He was the tallest of the crew as well as its flashpoint, always ready to go at anything hard at the drop of a hat. More than once, Blink had had to check him, pull his coat to the fact that violence was a last resort and the primary goal was to get that paper. However, his loyalty was on point and his gangsta unquestioned.

As he surveyed the scene, Jeff spotted honey from earlier. Her name was Keisha, and like she told him, she was wearing a white dress; he just didn't know she would wear it so well since she had been sitting in the driver seat when they met. Jeff had no idea ma was packing it like that. She had on a white one-strap Versace tube dress, and it hugged her curves like a second skin. Shorty was sitting on a gold mine with the fattest, roundest ass Jeff had ever seen, and as he watched her swaying to the beat, her ass moved like it had a mind of its own. Some buster was all up in her, trying to get some rhythm, but you can tell she wasn't feeling him as her eyes restlessly swept the crowd as if searching for someone. As soon as she saw him parting the crowd and heading her way, she gave a squeal of delight and rushed into his arms as if they'd been together forever. Jeff gave her a tight hug and whispered in her ear, "Damn, ma, I ain't know it was like that." Keisha gave him sly grin and did a 360-degree turn so he can take it all in.

"You like?" she asked in sultry voice.

"Hell yeah. C'mon, let's grab a table so we can get a few drinks." Jeff grabbed her by her hand to lead the way, never catching the daggers the buster who had been in her ear was shooting at him. The buster, whose name was Damion, followed the couple as they went to the high-backed lounge chairs to converse and drink. As they settled in, Damion approached and said, "My man, if this your bitch, then I guess you can pay me for all the drinks I brought before your ass got here." Jeff gave him a steely glare and said, "My man, two things. One, if you brought her anything to drink, you must have liked what you saw and was trying to get at her. You gambled and lost. Two, if you disrespect her or me again they're going to be carrying you outta here feet first."

He started to rise to his feet when Keisha placed a restraining hand on his chest and said to Damion, "I told this nigga I was waiting for somebody, but he insisted on buying those drinks. Here's your money back. Now like I told you, I can get my own." She reached in her purse to hand Damion two twenties, but he slapped it outta her hand, screaming, "Bitch, I ain't ask you for nothing. I was talking to this punk-ass nigga here," pointing at Jeff. As fast as a striking cobra,

Jeff grabbed the bottle of Patron off the table next to him and shattered it on top of Damion's head, sending him crashing to the floor. This was followed by three swift nose-crunching kicks to the face, causing the new Butters to become flecked with blood. By the time the bouncers arrived on the scene, Damion was sleeping peacefully on the floor. His two homies showed up a day late, having been on the dance floor and never witnessing the whole exchange. Now seeing their leader out like a light, they turned their murderous glares on Jeff, who stood ready for more battle.

Suddenly, Byrd stood next to him and shouted to the men, "What, y'all got a problem too? If it needs to go further, we can take it outside." Moon, Lil Harve, and Shiny flanked the duo on either side, so Damion's men just picked up their fallen leader and left. The bouncers then told Jeff and his crew that they would have to leave as well. After collecting Keisha's things and making sure they weren't walking into a trap outside, they all piled into Jeff's car. "Niggas can't never have a nice night out because some fool always don't know how to act," he mumbled.

Damion came to on the back seat of his own car where his henchmen had laid him, and as he put a hand to his forehead, he felt the golf ball-sized lump that had risen. "Fuck happened?" He asked as he looked around groggily, "Where the hell we at?" As his boy, Eagle rehashed to him the night's events, things came rushing back to him with a startling clarity. "Take me to Kenny. Those niggers are dead! Put their fucking hands on me? All of them are dead men walking!" Eagle turned the car toward the Lincoln Tunnel heading to Kenny's house, knowing that now they were about to go to war.

Kenny "Bear" Trestman was Damion's older brother by three years. He was also the major supplier to the Bronx and Queens, with an army of over three hundred soldiers waiting to do his bidding. The nickname was appropriate because he stood six feet and four inches and weighed a rock-solid 280 pounds, most of it in his chest, arms, and shoulders. As he watched Damion coming up the driveway with his crew in tow, he wondered what kind of shit he had gotten into now. He knew that Damion was a shit starter and lacked the heart and callousness of a true stomp-down soldier. But he was family, so Bear carried the extra weight and always made sure he was taken care of.

"Damn, nigger, what happened to you? Who gave you that softball on the side of your head?" he asked Damion as he stepped into the room.

"Some punk caught me sleeping and snuck me in the club tonight. Hit me from the blindside," Damion lied. "Said that since I was your brother that this was for you."

"So where the fuck was your backup while all this was going down?" bellowed Kenny. Eagle tried to melt into the wallpaper as Bear turned his murderous glare upon him.

"It all happened so fast nobody had a chance to react," interjected Damion, coming to Eagle's defense. Kenny was beside himself with anger. It was one thing to lay hands on his fam, quite another to threaten him.

"Who was this nigger?" he yelled.

"I'm not sure, but I think it was a couple niggers from Blink's crew," said Eagle. "They hang out over by the projects on 125th Street."

"Yeah, well, you niggers pack up; we got some work to put in tonight," said Bear as he rose.

He awoke with a start, immediately coherent and alert. The bed was drenched with sweat and the sheets tangled all around him. Images of the nightmare he had experienced remained vivid in his mind, understandably so because it was the same one over and over. In it, his daughter was pleading for him to help her, but he could never help because she remained tantalizingly just beyond his reach. She sank slowly deeper and deeper into the quagmire before she was lost forever from his sight.

"I'm so sorry, Denise. I let you down because I was not there to help. I just could not understand what it was you were going through," he whispered to himself.

Suddenly his feelings twisted from sorrow to a hot, burning desire for revenge, and he pushed himself up to take a shower as his mind prepared for the night ahead. As he toweled himself dry, another thought came to mind, and he decided that he'd better call in to his job before they reported him missing and came around to check on his whereabouts. He couldn't afford to be investigated by the authorities this late in the game. After he had completed his mission, it wouldn't matter; they could do whatever they wanted. But for now, he had so much to do. He picked up the phone and dialed in. After confirming that he had another week of personal leave to use, he assured his supervisor that he would be in the following Monday. This left just one more thing on his to-do list before he, again, became the hunter. The drive out to Caldwell Mental Facility was never something he looked forward to, not because of who he was going to see but rather the state he often found her in. It was located in upstate New York in a picturesque setting, so far from the outside world one would never guess at the horrors that lay within.

After the forty-five-minute drive, he checked in at the visitor's desk and was directed to room 415. As he entered the room, he saw her sitting on the edge of the bed, staring out the window, her eyes looking at but never really seeing the beautiful nature just beyond her walls. "Gladys," he whispered, gently taking her right hand in both of his and rubbing it. "How are you today, dear?" He neither received a response nor expected to; she hadn't spoken a word since that horrible day when they had found out that their little girl was dead. His wife had never recovered from her shock, her mind and soul retreating to a place that is beyond pain. To him, this was just another reason why vengeance was his to administer, one more thing *they* had to pay for. She neither smiled nor acknowledged his presence, so he just sat there as the darkness, once again, took over his soul. With a visible tremendous effort, he fought it back because he could not succumb to it here, not with her beside him. He turned and gave her a high-wattage smile, one that never reached his eyes.

After an hour more of stroking her hand and hair, he stood, bent to kiss her forehead, and said, "Well, good night, my love. I'll see you again in a few days." He then exited the room and closed the door quietly. Behind him, Gladys continued to stare at something only she could see.

After Jeff and his boys left the club, they pulled into the parking lot of the all-night diner on Amsterdam. Everybody was hyped up about tonight's earlier events, and they were the topic of discussion as they ordered their meals. While there, a group of hood rats came in talking loudly among themselves until they noticed the group of males and the single female accompanying them. Byrd, Moon, Lil Harve, and Shiny immediately snapped to attention as the women each had on a revealing outfit and were eying the men as if they were on the menu as well.

Byrd, ever the ladies' man, greeted them with a "Damn, I know y'all not gonna let us eat all this food we just ordered by ourselves, are you?"

"Of course not," replied the eldest of the group. "But don't you think we're gonna need a bigger table if we join you?" With that, the men immediately began rearranging furniture in the diner to accommodate their new number.

"Well, I see that you all have this covered," said Jeff. "So I'm gonna take Keisha and cut loose while y'all get familiar. Y'all okay getting home?"

"Oh, we got them faded," said the tallest female. "My name is Jade and that's my minivan parked outside. If they don't prove to be too lame, we'll make sure that they don't get home too late."

"Aight then, I'll catch y'all on the strip tomorrow," said Jeff, dapping his crew up before heading out the door.

"What about your food, my nigga?" asked Shiny.

"Oh, don't worry. I've got something for him to eat," said Keisha with a sexy grin as she led Jeff out the door.

*****

Blink was lying in bed with Kimmy, enjoying the afterglow that good lovemaking brings, her back pressed up to him as she enjoyed the gentle stroke of his fingers through her hair. He knew that, sooner or later, he was gonna have to make a commitment to this woman or just leave her alone altogether, and she had already made reference to this several times this evening. It wasn't as if he didn't have good intentions, nor was he the type to do a lot of bed-hopping. He just honestly did not feel that the kind of lifestyle he was living and what he was doing to make his money went with the "wife, kids, and white picket fence" ideology. He knew that at any minute, his whole world could come crashing down for any number of reasons, most notably arrest or death. Not only did he have 5-0 to worry about, but since he had stepped his game up, he had come to the notice of other crews who wanted his territory as well as the stickup boys. It was a 24-7 struggle to maintain his empire, so he had to make Kimmy understand that.

"Baby, I'm about to get up outta here. Hit Jeff up and make sure we're straight for business today."

"Oh, so that's it," she replied with mounting attitude. "We eat, we fuck, and then you're back out the door. I'm getting tired of this shit, Blink, and if that's all you have to offer, you can keep it moving."

Blink tried to keep a calm demeanor even though he felt himself heating up. "You know I got business to attend to. I can't make money and give you that good life by lying up in bed all day. What's wrong with you?"

"All I know is I ain't getting any younger," she shouted. "And if you expect me to wait for you for very much longer, then you've got another think coming."

"You know what," replied Blink, "I don't give a damn what you do. If you wanna roll, then roll, but I'm not gonna be arguing with you every time I got something to do. That's the problem with you females? When you got a good thing going, you don't realize it until it's gone. Fuck it, I'm out." He got up, put his clothes on, and slammed the door on his way out, never paying attention to the lamp that shattered against it behind him.

After waiting for Blink's crew to show up at their strip for half the night, Bear and his boys were back at it first thing in the morning. They had gotten word that Blink's crew normally opened up shop around 10:00 a.m., so they sat in three black vans around the corner just clock-watching. Of them that sat fingering their weapons, Damion seethed the most because he had never truly gotten over being knocked out in front of his boys. He figured you lead by example, and what kind of example was he setting by being rocked to sleep? He sat in the lead vehicle with his brother, his gaze alternating

22

between the clock and the block ahead. Bear peeped this and said, "Be cool, man. You're gonna fuck around and fire that thing off in here by mistake the way you're finger fucking that trigger. You'll be able to get yours back once these niggers show." Damion looked over at him but said nothing, just kept stroking the MP5 he held on his lap.

As Blink cruised down Washington Avenue, his fingers drummed on the steering wheel along to the beat of Jay Z's latest hit. He grabbed his cell phone and dialed Jeff's number. "Yo, what's up, my man? Y'all niggers got shit on and popping over there yet?"

"Naw, my nigga. Them hoochies they hooked up with last night were all the way live, so we getting a late start. Don't sweat it though. I'm on my way to get Moon and Lil Harve, and Shine said they'd open up shop for us in about fifteen minutes," Jeff replied.

"Aight, I should be there myself in about half an hour, so I'll catch up with you on the block. Out." With that, Blink cut the connection and thought about his trip back to DC to see Nut tomorrow.

The sniper sat low in the Honda Civic he had stolen from a lot earlier. He didn't want to chance the Ford again just in case Blink recognized it from the episode near his mother's house. He saw the three identical black vans idling down the street and wondered what their business was here but dismissed them as he knew the vehicles of the main players on Blink's team by sight. None of them pushed a van, black or otherwise. He had already decided that today would be the day he struck as his anger and thirst for revenge had risen since his visit with his wife.

At 10:00 a.m. sharp, Bear saw the block suddenly come alive with activity. It's as if the fiends rose up out of the sidewalks as they began to line up to purchase a bag of that high-grade smack Blink's boys were pushing. Harve and Shiny arrived on the scene and gave packages for some of their runners to distribute. As Damion laid eyes on Shiny, he recognized him as one of the goons with Jeff at the club and his heart rate accelerated rapidly.

"There go one of those niggers right there," he whispered even though he couldn't be heard outside the van. "And I think that other nigger was with them too."

"Are you sure?" asked Bear, his gaze narrowing on the two men he saw handing out packages.

"Yeah, I'm sure, nigga! Let's go twist these clowns' caps back." In his desire for revenge, Damion neglected to wait until his main target appeared. He just wanted to spread hurt, and it didn't much matter who got it. Bear gave the signal to the other two vans behind him, and they proceeded down the street.

The sniper watched with renewed interest as the vans rolled by him. He knew instantly that something was up, and wasn't surprised when he saw the windows and the side doors of the van open up. He could see the barrels of the weapons extended from the vehicles, and he knew what was about to happen. As the lead van drew abreast of the crowd, it was as if WWIII had started on the streets of NY. All you could hear were the sounds of automatic weapons going off as the deadly wall of lead tore through fiends and pushers alike. The sound was deafening as the frantic screams of the fleeing crowd turned into moans of pain as men and women alike were shot down where they stood.

Shiny, the main target, never stood a chance. He took a full blast from a shotgun, his body jerking and dancing as the bullets tore through his chest. Dead before he hit the ground, he lay staring with unseeing eyes at the package of dope sitting just beyond his grasp, one hand clutching the pistol at his waist he never got a chance to use. Lil Harve did manage to get his Glock out and fire a few shots toward their tormentors, but they all missed as he was backing away, trying to find cover. As he ducked down into the stairwell leading into the apartment, he felt a red-hot poker stick him in his back, and he stumbled for a few steps before the soothing darkness claimed him. The last thing he heard was the squeal of rubber as the vans raced away after leaving their deadly message, the carnage left behind for all to see.

As Jeff neared the block, he saw the vans racing past him in the other direction and saw Damion's contorted face in the passenger's window of the first one. *If that clown is around here, I know he's up to no good*, he thought to himself. He pulled his .45 caliber from under his seat and placed it next to his leg. When he turned the corner to his block, his mouth dropped open in horror. The bodies of fourteen men and women lay riddled in pools of blood in different poses, some missing complete limbs and a couple with their faces gone. Worse of all, he could clearly see the body of his road dawg Shiny as he lay with his neck twisted at a grotesque angle, knowing immediately that he was dead. Still, Jeff ran to him and, after feeling for but failing to find a pulse, gently closed his eyes. "Rest in peace, bro, and go into the next world knowing that the niggers who did this are only one step behind you. That's my word," he said.

As the sounds of the sirens became louder in the distance, he heard a groan from the stairwell and crept toward it to peer over the ledge. He saw Harve lying in a pool of blood, gun close at hand. He bounded down the steps and gathered Harve up as he would a child and ran as fast as he could to his car. "Hang in there, man. Just stay with me. I'mma get you to a hospital faster than these honkies will. Just stay with me," he begged as he laid Harve across the rear seats and jumped behind the wheel, speeding off with little regard to the traffic behind him. As he drove, he called Blink's cell, and he answered on the second ring. "Yo, wassup, B?"

"I told you I was on my way."

"It ain't even about that," cried Jeff. "Man, the spot been hit and we've suffered casualties. Shine is dead, and I got Harve in my car headed to Memorial Hospital. I don't know if he's gonna make it."

"What?" said Blink, not believing his ears. "Man, I'm like ten minutes from the hospital. I'll meet you there. Don't say anything else over the phone." Blink hung up and did a 180-degree U-turn, pointing the Lex back the way it had come. At Forty-Seventh and Manor, he hooked a left turn, and three minutes later pulled up in the hospital's parking lot.

He hopped out of the car and raced through the emergency entrance doors, shouting at the receptionist to get the hell off the phone and get a prep team ready as they were about to receive a gunshot victim. The receptionist regarded him with trepidation as she saw no gunshot victim with him nor had she received any call stating that one was on the way. She decided that the best thing to do would be to call security to have this crazy man escorted out of here. Just as she was about to pick up the phone, she heard the screech of brakes outside the door, and seconds later, a bloodied Jeff burst into the room, screaming for help. Seeing him covered in blood, she immediately assumed that he was the shooting victim and directed the descending medical team toward him. Jeff had to shout to be heard, "Get off me, you stupid mu'fuckas. The victim is in my car outside."

Finally, the head doctor realized what was going on and rushed his medical team through the doors. Seconds later, they came back with Lil Harve strapped to a gurney and disappeared through the doors leading to the operation room. Jeff and Blink attempted to follow their fallen comrade but were stopped by the solidly built nurse who blocked their path. "Sorry, gentlemen, but you are not allowed access to the OR. You may wait in the visiting room until someone comes for you, and you'll be advised of your friend's condition as soon as it is prudent to do so," she said. With that, she spun on her heels and disappeared through the doors.

"What the fuck happened?" Blink asked Jeff as soon as they were alone. "Who did this shit?"

Jeff, realizing that he was standing there covered in Harve's blood and therefore likely to be questioned rather intensely, said, "C'mon, let's roll up outta here so I can get cleaned up. Looking like I do now, 5-0 is sure to take me downtown. I'll fill you in on the way, and we can come back to check on Harve." They both piled in Jeff's car as he headed to his crib. Jeff filled Blink in on everything, starting from the fight in the club up to recognizing Damion's face in the van. "It had to be them niggers. We ain't got beef with nobody else. We have to get everybody together for a meeting," said Blink. "Where is Moon?"

"I don't know. When I stopped to scoop him up, his mom told me that he wasn't at home. Now that you mention it, it sure seems strange because I told him last night what time I'd be through today, and now he's a no-show. How them niggers know where we hang our hats at and what time we open shop?" Jeff wondered out loud. His mind began to form suspicions because, to him, everyone but Blink and Harve were suspect in the death of his dawg Shiny. Someone had to pay, and pay dearly they would.

*****

The sniper sat up straight as he witnessed the destruction and chaos the vans brought. Such a wanton and callous disregard for life was beyond even his imagination. Sure, he was a killer, but he only killed those who deserved to die, he mused. The gunmen before his eyes killed the guilty and the innocent alike because, in his view, the users and fiends were only victims of the pushers. They didn't deserve to be gunned down because of their weaknesses. They fell victim to the same disease that claimed his daughter, so he believed them worthy of the same vengeance he sought for her. As each van passed the block and spewed forth its fatal barrage, he started up his engine and began to tail them. He followed at a discreet distance, and to his surprise, the caravan in front didn't seem to be in any particular hurry, as if they'd just come from a family outing in the park. They cruised through the heart of the city through Lincoln Tunnel and eventually entered the northern part of the county where the houses were few and far between. Only the monied lived here, where in each driveway sat a Porsche, BMW, Benz, or some other luxury vehicle. The lawns were well manicured and the houses huge, with pools in each yard that had gardeners and maintenance men scurrying to and fro.

The vans pulled up to a high-walled gated mansion with a guard that sat in a booth who opened the gates for the vans to pass. As the gates shut behind the caravan, the sniper continued up the street to what appeared to be a sitting park, complete with swings, seesaws, a merry-go-round and several picnic tables. He turned around in the cul-de-sac and pulled to the curb. Removing his binoculars, he studied the layout of the estate where the vans had disappeared. To his way of thinking, this group had replaced Blink's on his list as he believed Blink's had been severely crippled by the attack and were no longer a priority. The ferocity displayed by this crew made them a clear and present danger, and therefore they needed to be immediately eliminated. He couldn't discern any movement as the windows to the mansion appeared to be shrouded with heavy drapes concealing the activity within. This only increased his belief that they were sinister, so he made note of the number of armed guards patrolling the grounds and the intervals at which they made their rounds. With the address written down, he made his exit. He had some investigating to do himself because he had no idea who resided at this castle. However, he had his ways of finding out, and once he did, he would return. He was, after all, a creature of the night, and the night would come again. So would he.

Inside, Damion whooped and yelled as the celebration began.

"Boy, did you see those fools falling? I put in some serious work out there today. I bet they'll think twice about who they put their hands on from now on," he crowed.

His team of goons celebrated with him as the Henny and Goose flowed and the Blunts were rolled and passed. Ironhead, the driver of the last van, peeked out the window and saw a Honda Civic turn the corner, heading out. He briefly wondered if he had seen that car behind them on their way here, but he quickly dismissed that thought as the car was too nondescript and the driver too old to be of any consequence. Besides, if he didn't get back into the game room, he would miss out on the liquor and weed, and who knows, maybe Bear would send for some big butt strippers as a reward for a job well-done.

"Yo, man, let me put some fire to that," he yelled at Eagle as he headed back to the party.

*****

Blink sat at the head of the large wooden table in the abandoned warehouse his crew used as a meeting place on occasion. Around him, seven chairs were occupied by the main lieutenants and enforcers of his team. Two chairs remained empty, tipped to lean against the table so there was no mistaking the meaning. They belonged to Shiny and Harve, their absence speaking louder than words. "I guess, by now, all of you have heard what went down today. We lost a good soldier, a great man, and a better friend, one who was here since the beginning. Randy, I want you to make sure his family is taken care of. Get money from the kitty to pay for the funeral and make sure that his moms and little sister want for nothing. Now I know that all of you are burning for some payback," he said, eyes coming to rest particularly on Jeff. "But we've got to play it smart. First of all, we have to find out who it was that hit us. We have a face, now we've got to put a name to it. Jeff and Moon, I need y'all to ask around at that club about who it was y'all had that beef with. But be on the low low with it. We trying to dig up this info on the QT. The rest of you, I want you to get your teams prepped and ready 'cause when we hit, we're gonna hit hard and fast. Any questions?"

"Yeah," Moon spoke up. "What are you gonna be doing while we're taking care of this?"

Blink recalled Jeff's earlier suspicions of Moon, so his response was careful and guarded. "That's on a need-to-know basis, and since you don't need, you don't have to know," he said.

"All right, if that's all y'all head on out, I'll meet up with you back here around nine tonight. Jeff, before you leave, let me holler at you."

Jeff, whose face still looked like a threatening storm cloud, waited until everyone had left and then looked at Blink.

"What's up, boss?"

"My man, I'm gonna need you to hold this down while I'm gone. I have to make that run to see Nut so I can hit him off and see what I can do on the re-up tip. We got to keep this thing moving so we won't lose what we've already established, plus we have to pay our workers. While I'm gone, you're in charge, so put our product back out there two blocks over by the Paca Street building. We can use Shirley's apartment for the stash. She's already on our payroll, so she'll know what's up. Lastly, I want you to send somebody over to the hospital to check on Lil Harve. I don't want you to go yourself because you might be recognized from this morning, and I don't need 5-0 holding you. Okay?"

"You got it, Blink. Just one thing, though, man. Who gonna watch your back in Chocolate City? I'd rather roll with you because you know we ride or die if niggers try to get out of pocket," Jeff said.

Blink smiled as his heart was touched by this show of love and loyalty. "I know that's real, my nigga, and that's why I feel you in here," he said while touching his chest. "I've got to just trust and believe that my nigga Nut ain't on no shady shit because I'm gonna need you here in case something does goes wrong. I'll hit you on your hip to keep you up on what's happening. And oh yeah, I see what you're feeling about Moon. Keep an eye on him and see how he's acting. Vibes ain't right, man."

"No doubt," said Jeff. "I'll catch up with you later tonight, One B."

Blink called Nut to let him know that he'd be there in a couple of hours and that he would hit him once he got to the outskirts. As he fought through the bumper-to-bumper traffic headed to I 95 South, he took stock of the situation and how he wanted to handle it. For real he didn't want to kill anyone; he was just trying to make a dollar the best way he knew how. But he knew that he couldn't let Shine's death go unavenged; not only would he lose the respect of the crew, but he also wouldn't be able to look himself in the mirror. He and Shine covered a lot of ground together, and when he caught that eighteen-month bid, it was Shine who held him down, acting as the go-between to make sure he had everything he needed. He had been Jeff's right-hand man and relayed the orders Blink gave to Jeff. One thing was for certain: if Jeff found the ones who did this, not even Blink could hold him back. After about three and a half hours, he entered into the Maryland borders and pulled over to a service station to gas up. He called Nut to let him know he'd arrive at the meeting point in about forty-five minutes and glanced at the briefcase in the back seat. He cracked it open to reveal $90,000 stacked in bands of hundred-dollar bills, and he had in his duffel bag another $150,000 to purchase ten more bricks. There was no need for consignment this time because now a nigga was paid. He paid the attendant, slid back into his seat, and headed south to meet his connect.

This time, Nut was in the back of a dove gray Maybach that glistened so brightly you had a hard time looking directly at it. As Blink pulled in the parking lot, Nut slid out the back seat and walked over. "Damn, nigg," Blink said while admiring the $200,000 vehicle. "You doing it like that?"

"I gotta be me," replied Nut while exchanging pounds and hugs with Blink. "Ain't no need in making it if you're not gonna enjoy it, know what I mean? Hey, where your man at?"

"I had to leave him at home to captain the ship," said Blink. 'We had some shit go down that's gonna require our full and undivided attention, and I needed him to handle business until I got back." Blink proceeded to put Nut down with the daylight shootings back home.

"Man, that was your crew that got sprayed? That shit made the news all the way down here. Well, why the fuck you down here now? This shit could have waited."

"Hey, a deal is a deal is a deal," replied Blink. "A man's word is his bond, and I would go through hell and high water to keep mine."

"See, that's why I fucks with you," Nut said. "Most people would've used that as an excuse as to why they couldn't make it. But here you are, big as day."

"Speaking of which, I got something for you," Blink replied, reaching for the briefcase. "Here's the 90 grand I owe you for the first load, and I've got 150 g's for ten more of them thangs if we're still swinging like that."

"Always for you, B. You know you my peoples, so ain't nothing to it. Hop in your whip and follow me out to my crib so I can hit you up something proper. It's only about fifteen minutes away."

"Aight, I'm right behind you." Nut had his driver take it slow because he knew Blink was unfamiliar to the DC area and its one-way streets, and it's easy to get turned around or lost because of these. They came to a stop in front of a gorgeous brownstone in the affluent neighborhood of Georgetown, where the ritzy shops and restaurants for people of means were. As both vehicles pulled into the four-car garage, the door automatically shut behind them, shutting out any prying eyes. Blink followed Nut through the side entrance, followed closely by Nut's huge bodyguard, and as he stepped through the door it was like stepping into a picture from *House and Gardens* magazine. Nut's townhouse was absolutely stunning. The living room was sunken at least eight feet and done in an earthly beige color with a sofa that looked like it could seat at least twenty people stretched against the far wall. Directly across from it was the biggest television screen Blink had ever seen. It had to be custom-made because it was at least 140 inches wide. The plush chocolate-colored carpet was so thick your shoes disappeared when you stepped on it.

Around the walls, several very authentic-looking paintings hung and different African artifacts adorned the coffee and end tables. Blink's mouth must have been open because Nut chuckled and said, "It ain't nothing homey, make yourself at home. The bar is over there, and there's beer in the fridge." As Blink crossed over to the bar to get a shot of Henny, Nut clicked the remote and the screen jumped to life. The Redskins were playing the Cowboys, and it seemed to Blink that he was at the stadium itself. The surround sound system was killer. Nut proceeded into the rear of the house and entered a code, and the bookshelf in the corner slide back to reveal a recessed wall. Opening the compartment, Nut stepped back to admire the rows upon rows of stacked and banded cash amid the gleaming white array of neatly stacked kilos. He removed ten and stuck them in an oversized gym bag from his closet, closed the compartment back up, and clicked the remote again. The bookshelf slid noiselessly back into place.

"Here you are, my man," Nut said as he tossed the gym bag to Blink. "Ten keys of pure. Make sure it's cut up good or you're gonna have a bunch of dead fiends on your hands."

"I've got that covered," said Blink. "I have some of the best steppers in the game, and they'll make these ten keys into pure heaven for the heads without losing one of them." He sat the duffel bag on the table and opened the zipper.

"It's 150 g's, just like I said. It's all yours." Nut gave a slight head nod, and his bodyguard stepped forward, grabbed the duffel, and disappeared into the back. "On another note, Blink, if you need any help with that other thing you've got going on up in the Apple, you know that all you got to do is ask," stated Nut. "You're one of my most reliable outlets, and I protect those who are good with me. I have over two hundred of the most stomped-down soldiers alive, and it ain't nothing but a ride to us. Just say the word."

"Boy, I appreciate that more than you know and if I need you, I'll definitely holler. But right now, this is more personal than business, so I feel the need to be hands-on for this one. Shit, get to be more than I can handle I'll be at you though."

"Aight, One. You be careful going back up the highway. Smokey be all over 95 this time of the day."

"I appreciate the love," Blink said as he again exchanged hugs and daps with Nut. Nut gave one last wave as Blink backed out of the garage and disappeared back into the house. Blink pulled over at a diner to get something to eat and program his GPS to lead him out of this maze and back to 95. He prayed that his journey north would be uneventful since he already had more than enough on his plate to deal with. After finishing off his meal of cheesesteak, french fries, and iced tea, he paid his bill, left a ten-dollar tip—which earned him a high-wattage smile from the exhausted-looking waitress—and headed out the door.

Jeff and Moon pulled up in front of Club Shake Off, which, at this hour, wasn't open but had several different deliveries going on as the staff prepared for what they hoped would be a busy night. Since he was a main participant in the fight the other night he hoped he wouldn't be recognized be anyone. Normally he would have just sent Moon in to get info, but he still remained highly suspicious of him. They would go in together, and he'd just take his chances. Fortunately, he was able to intercept one of the liquor deliverymen on his way in. "Hey, bro, how you doing?" Jeff asked in a cheery voice. "Me and my man here are from Philly. We're in town for a couple of days and looking for a spot to shine at tonight. How are the happenings up in here?"

The deliveryman looked as if he was glad to have someone to talk to. "Well, you came to the right spot, guy. By about ten, there'll be so much ass up in here you'll have your head on a swivel," he chuckled.

"I hear that," Jeff replied. "I was told that there be mad honeys up in here on a regular. But look, we ain't for no trouble and I heard niggas be wildin' out in this spot. I heard that the other night y'all damn near had a riot breakout."

"Naw, man, that was just that fool Damion always trying to act like a tough guy. He figures that since Bear is his brother, he owns the place. They ought to just ban him from here, but his brother spends mad loot in here so he gets a pass. But he got what he had coming the other night. Some nigga knocked his ass out cold. Wish I knew who it was so I could shake his hand."

"Are you talking about Bear that has Brownsville and Bed Stuy on lock? queried Jeff.

"Yeah, the one and the same. Calls himself Mr. Untouchable since he has such a large crew. He'll get his too one of these days. Look, man, I'd love to stay and chat with you, but I gotta get this done. I still have three more stops to make. Maybe I'll see you up in here tonight."

"Yeah, yeah," Jeff mused. "Thanks for the heads-up. If you see me tonight, holler at me. First rounds on me." He and Moon headed back to his car, his mind churning with the information he'd just received. He knew all too well who Kenny "Bear" Trestman was. He'd done time with him over on the island and had watched him come up from a distance. Rumor had it that he was connected with the Italian mob and moved pretty much most of the dope from New York to Miami. Supposed to have a team of killers but still liked to put in the work himself. He didn't know that Damion was his brother, but it didn't matter anyway. Jeff bowed down to no man regardless of what his reputation or status was, and nobody could disrespect him or his and walk away. He did, however, know that they had to be careful with their next move, and when they did hit, they had to hit hard. He noticed how quiet Moon had been during the exchange and nudged him with his elbow.

"Wassup, nigga, you ain't have no questions for dude back there?"

"Naw, man, I was following your lead. It looked like you had everything well in hand." Moon replied. Jeff's eyes narrowed. "You know, you never did tell me where you were when I came to scoop you on the day all of this went down."

"Oh, I thought I mentioned that I had to go to Ryker's to visit my uncle. If I'd known, I would most definitely had been there busting my gat," Moon replied unconvincingly.

Jeff tested him further. "Yeah, well, we'll see. We're gonna ride on them clowns tonight, and I hope your gunplay is as good as your mouth."

Jeff noticed the nervous sideways glance Moon gave him but kept further comments to himself. *This busta sho nuff bears watching,* he thought. *I got him faded, though.*

Out loud, he said, "Well, c'mon, let's swing past the hospital to check out Harve. Blink should be back soon and then we can plan this thing out." No sooner were the words out of his mouth than his phone rang, flashing Blink's name across the screen. 'Well, speak of the devil and who should appear," he said as he answered it. "Yo, what's up, my nigga? Everything good?"

"Hell yeah. I'm about an hour and a half away, and I got half of Columbia with me," he crowed, speaking in code. "Round up the folks and meet me at the new stash house around four thirty."

"Will do, baby. I got the info we were searching for, so I definitely have to pull your coat to a few things. Right now, we're getting ready to check on Harve, but we'll see you then."

"Aight, One." Jeff broke the connection as Moon asked who was on the phone. Some sixth sense told him to share as little as possible, so he played it off as if it were nothing. "Just something I've got to take care of a little later on," Jeff said. The rest of the ride was made in silence as both men dealt with the thoughts going through their heads.

When they reached the hospital, they had a twenty-minute wait because Lil Harve already had the maximum number of visitors allowed at one time. As they sat in the waiting room, Moon said, "I'll be back. I gotta go drain the lizard." He hopped up and scurried down the hall to the men's room. After entering, he peeped under each stall to make sure he was alone and then pulled out his cell and punched in some numbers.

"Yo, what's good?" growled the voice on the other end. "I hope you're calling with some info and not just wasting my fucking time."

"Naw, man, I got the 411. We all are gonna meet at the new stash house I told you about. That nigga Jeff thought he was slick, but he ain't know I could hear his whole conversation. You ain't forgot what you promised me, have you?"

"Naw, bitch ass, I ain't forgot. After we take care of that buncha clowns, I'mma let you take over that territory long as you don't forget who the big dawg is."

"Never that," said Moon. "I'mma holler at you when we're on our way. Later." He clicked off and opened the stall door and almost shit his pants. Standing there staring evilly at him was Jeff.

"Who the fuck was you talking to, nigga?"

"Uh ... I ... uh, nobody," stammered Moon. "I was just checking on my mom, letting her know I'd be home late so she wouldn't have a plate waiting on me."

"And for that you had to go huddle up in a stall?" Jeff questioned.

"Yeah, I figured while I was taking a shit, I'd handle that too."

"I thought you said you had to piss, nigger, plus I ain't hear no toilet flush?"

"It was a false alarm," Moon improvised. "I musta just had gas. Plus, why you all up on me, Jeff?" asked Moon.

Jeff studied him for a minute and then said, "My bad, nigga. A brother's just on edge with all this shit that's happening. C'mon, we can go see Harve. While you were in here, his family came downstairs and left. His mom is a wreck."

"Aight, let's go," Moon sighed. He believed he had just gotten away with the closest call of his life because he knew that if Jeff had any idea what he was up to, he'd snuff him in a minute. Moon had long had designs on Blink's position simply because jealousy ate away at his heart and he had no loyalty. He had often lain awake at night, scheming on ways to have him removed, and then this opportunity had fallen into his lap. As he followed behind Jeff in the hall, he stared at the back of his head with hateful eyes. *Your turn is coming real soon too, bitch*, he thought.

# CHAPTER 4

The sniper had his resources check on the occupants of the big-walled mansion he had tailed them to, and his eyes widened as he read the results. Kenny Trestman was number 15 on his list, his name surrounded by stars and asterisks. And that was because he'd tried to save the best for last. Kenny, or Bear as he was better known, was the big fish in the pond. He was suspected of so much murder and mayhem that the sniper believed the crime rate would go down 50 percent with his arrest or removal from this life. Further, he had long since suspected that Kenny was the source who supplied the drugs that had killed his little girl.

Denise had been a delicate flower, easily impressionable; and when the then-fledgling drug lord wooed her with his fancy cars, jewelry, and big bankroll, she was caught up like a piece of flotsam in a whirlwind. It didn't help his conscience that he was too busy at the time with his job to sacrifice and save her, but his wife was also powerless against the lure of the good life for Denise. Before his eyes, he saw her spiraling out of control until that fateful day the phone call arrived, informing them that her body had been found in a shooting gallery in Queens. How naive they were to not even recognize the all too apparent signs of drug use! If he hadn't been so caught up in his career, his little girl would be alive today, and now God had given him the opportunity for payback. He would be the instrument of destruction, the weapon used by the Almighty to strike down this minion of Satan, who was poisoning people across the buroughs. And it would start tonight. He headed down to the basement to prepare for war.

# CHAPTER 5

As Jeff led Moon into Harve's hospital room, he was shocked by the sight that greeted him. His man was hooked up to so many machines, with various tubes and lines running in and out of his body, that he looked like an experiment gone wrong. Jeff neared the bed where Lil Harve lay with his eyes closed, straining his eyes to see the rise and fall of his chest. Tears stung his eyes as he fought to keep from crying. Witnessing his people so helpless brought back the rage and frustration he had suppressed. Moon hung in the background, conspicuous by his lack of sorrow or anger. Harve was supposed to be his family too, but Moon was acting like that was a total stranger lying there.

"Hey, my cell phone has gone dead," said Jeff. "Let me hold yours so I can call Blink to let him know we're here and how Harve is doing." When Moon handed his phone over, Jeff crossed the room to one of the chairs, the phone held out of Moon's view. Jeff hit redial and the last number Moon had dialed jumped to the screen. With a poker face hiding the murderous feelings he felt rising within, Jeff read the numbers and the name Bear to himself, knowing they had a traitor in their midst. He dialed Blink's number to deflect any suspicion on Moon's part and updated him as to Harve's condition. When Blink asked why he was calling from Moon's phone, Jeff replied that he would pull his coat when they hooked up. When Jeff handed the phone back to Moon, he glanced at the screen and put it back in his pocket, none the wiser about what just went down. Jeff said, "C'mon, Blink's almost back. We got just enough time to meet him at the spot." He pressed two fingers to his lips, placed them on them on Harve's forehead, and spun on his heels out the door.

Blink pulled up at Shirley's apartment at four. He had a half hour to kill before Jeff was due to meet him, so he locked his car and took the steps up to the third floor. He was already mentally scoping out spots where he would place his runners and lookouts, but he would have a better picture once he reconnoitered the rooftops. The hallways were dimly lit and smelled strongly of piss, mingled with the all too familiar smells of the different meals being prepared inside each apartment. He would make sure that these residents made a come-up also; that was the secret to his success and longevity. Make the people happy with the simple things, and they would never snitch on you. First though, he had to make sure Shirley was home and still down for the move.

He knocked on room 317 and could hear someone shuffling to the door to peer through the peephole. A few seconds later, he heard the many locks and chains being removed and the door was thrown open by Shirley. "Well, well," she smirked, "look what the cat dragged in. I thought you had forgotten all about our arrangements and found another spot for your move." Shirley stepped back so Blink could enter and closed the door behind him. She greeted him with a hug so tight that if he had been thirty pounds lighter, she would have cracked his ribs. Shirley was just a big woman. Standing three inches taller than him and about one hundred pounds heavier, she made him feel tiny by comparison. In her day, she was known as the queen gangsta, pimping out a stable of eight girls and slinging everything from weed to smack. If Shirley didn't have it, she knew where to get it.

High living and a taste for her own product eventually brought her down, and she did a serious stretch in the Feds. However, she was still a formidable force to be reckoned with. "Naw, Shirl," Blink replied as soon as he gathered his breath. "You'll just have to make a few moves to get straight again. I know you've heard about what happened the other day on my strip."

"Yeah that was some fucked-up shit," Shirley said. "Let them niggas try coming up in here like that. I got something for them." She reached over behind the couch and pulled out a fully automatic double-barreled shotgun, capable of firing eight loads of twelve-gauge buckshot before having to reload.

"It ain't even gonna come to that, Shirl. You know I'mma handle that when the time is right. Bad boys move in silence."

"I know that's right, nigga, and I know you're gangsta. I just want you to know your product is protected."

"I already know that, Shirl. That's why I chose you. Pops used to talk about you all the time, and I know the two of you did some business together back in the day. Plus, I'm gonna send over two shooters to watch your back as well. Do you have the mixers and baggers lined up?"

"Hell yeah, that's all been taken care of. I've got five of the best cutters in the business waiting for me. All I was doing was waiting for your call."

"Well, hit 'em up and tell them to get here. The product is downstairs, and I'll bring it up as soon as Jeff gets here. He's on his way and should pull up in fifteen minutes or so."

"Aight, Blink, I'm on it."

"Here's your cut for the first week's pay," said Blink, handing Shirley twenty one hundred–dollar bills. "Tell your cutters they each get $700 a week, but they know what's gonna happen if we catch 'em being light-fingered."

"Hell, man," Shirley growled. "If I catch them stealing, it won't be nothing left of them for you to do anything with. Bitches know better."

"Aight, then we set. See you in a few." With that, Blink headed back downstairs.

Jeff pulled up while Blink was sitting in his car, listening to some old Biggie. Both men got out to hug each other as Moon slid out the passenger side, looking all around. "Boy, glad to see you back in one piece," Jeff greeted Blink. "You been on my mind the whole time you were gone."

"Things couldn't have gone any better," replied Blink. "My man Nut is a true stomp comrade, and it was all love from the jump."

"Wish I could say the same for the home front," whispered Jeff while directing a meaningful glance toward Moon. Blink caught the look and instantly knew what the play was.

"Well, let's go up and holler at Shirley before we take this work to her," Blink said. "Moon, you might as well come too. See what the setup is."

"Naw, man, I'll just stay out here while you two handle that. I'll make sure the product stays safe while you're gone," Jeff said.

"Moon, I didn't hear my man put that to you as a question. That was an order. Now get your bluffing ass on up here."

Not wanting to arouse suspicion, Moon followed the men into the building, not knowing when Bear and his team were gonna make their move. He definitely didn't want to be caught up in the crossfire and be accidentally gunned down by Bear's goons, but he didn't see a way out. This time, the three men used the elevator and got off on the third floor. Blink again knocked on Shirley's door, and it opened immediately. Jeff and Moon followed him inside. As soon as the door closed, Jeff pulled his nine and pointed it directly at Moon's head. "Fuck you doing, man, pointing that thing at me? What kinda games are you playing?"

"Naw, nigga, what kinda games are you playing?" Jeff echoed as he reached into Moon's pocket with one hand and removed Moon's cell phone. He handed it to Blink. "Go to outgoing calls. Guess whose number that is right behind yours?"

Moon felt his heart sink into his shoes. He instantly knew that he had been busted, and his eyes darted right and left as he searched for a way out. Jeff spoke to Blink, his eyes never leaving Moon's face, "We found out today who it was who hit us. The name of the nigga I rocked is Damion, and his brother happens to be Bear Trestman, the dude who has half this city on lock. Evidently, our friend here has been feeding him info on us, which explains how they knew where and at what time we could be touched as we opened up shop."

Moon yelled in desperation, "You've got it all wrong, man. I got his number because I was only trying to get us another connect once ours started drying up! You gotta believe me, Blink."

"Lying bitch-ass nigga!" Jeff shouted. "I heard your whole fucking conversation when you were in the bathroom at the hospital. You gave those bastards everything, and they're probably on their way now to hit us again. You're the reason Shine is dead and Harve's in that damned hospital bed!"

Shirley sucked her teeth. "Ain't nothing worse than a snitching bitch-ass traitor," she said. "Putting your own people in harm's way. How low can you go? Want me to do him for you Blink?"

"Naw, we ain't got time for that right now," said Blink. "Put some duct tape around this nigga's hands, feet, and mouth. We gotta get you outta this spot, Shirley, because niggas probably on their way to air it out now. First, give me this." Blink ripped Moon's gun from his waist. "You won't be needing this anymore. Jeff, take this bitch downstairs and put him in the car. I got a few calls to make. Take him to the warehouse and put a few people on him. We'll still meet there with the rest of the crew at seven as planned. After you take care of that, come back here. I got a surprise in store for Bear and his boys."

*****

Bear and his caravan were, at that very moment, loading up for the ride across town to eliminate Blink and the rest of his crew. This time, they would travel in four stolen cars, vehicles not recognizable by Blink's team and unable to be traced back to them. He had four of his heaviest and most trusted hitters in each ride, each one of them strapped to the gills. He and Damion rode in the lead car with his two best bodyguards, plus a driver. If Moon's info was correct, then Blinks' crew would be just arriving at the stash house and would probably be there for a while, getting things organized. He had tried to call that fool a few times, but his phone kept going straight to voicemail. No matter, if he got in the line of fire, they'd wet his ass up too. He had an eye on Blink's territory for sometime now. It was in a lucrative part of the city, and now was the time to claim it. After tonight, he would surely be the king of New York, and then he'd have these Italians coming to him for favors, not the other way around.

After everyone checked their weapons, one last time the killers got underway on their mission of death.

*****

The sniper watched the caravan head out one behind the other, and he wondered what kind of mayhem they were planning this time. No matter because he was determined that this would be Bear's last ride. As he again followed behind at a discreet distance, he thought about his daughter and his promise to her. "Retribution is at hand, sweetheart. The hour of vengeance draws near." He gripped the steering wheel tighter in anticipation and even considered just pulling up next to the lead car and spraying everyone inside. He discarded that plan because he knew that would only lead to a shootout with Bear's soldiers, and his chances of escape would be minimal. Not that he was afraid of death, he just still had so much work to do after this one was over. He would play it by ear and see when the best chance presented itself and then go from there. He had always been great at improvising.

As Bear's convoy pulled up down the street from the stash house, he surveyed the area through his binoculars. Moon's info was on point because he could see both Blink's and Jeff's vehicles parked in front of the building. Two of their runners lounged on the corner, waiting to serve the fiends as they came up. He figured to take them by surprise, storming into the building and overwhelming them by sheer force of numbers and firepower. He gave the command to proceed, and the vehicles zipped up and screeched to a stop in front of the building, two in front and two behind. Bear, Damion, and the bodyguards jumped out of the lead car brandishing automatics and bounding up the steps. Before he reached the front door, he was greeted by a cheerful voice that seemed to come from everywhere.

"Hey, Bear, long way from home, aren't you?" Blink shouted down from the rooftop across the street. With that, he opened up with the MP5 he had gripped in his hands, and guns appeared at every window, all shooting at Bear and his crew. They were absolutely cut to ribbons as his men and their cars alike were riddled with bullets. He dove through the glass front door in an effort to escape the murderous fusillade and turned around to help Damion get out of the line of fire. As he turned, he was greeted by the sight of Damion's head being blown completely off his shoulders, courtesy of a direct hit from both barrels of a twelve-gauge. His lifeless body swooned and rolled into the gutter while his head landed fifteen feet away, its mouth bared open in a grotesque parody of a smile.

"No!" shouted Bear as he struggled to get up from his shelter. His one remaining bodyguard managed to keep him down as he watched his hit team disappear before his eyes.

Hearing the sounds of approaching sirens, Blink gave the signal to vacate the premises, and his crew retreated from their hiding places. The damage they had inflicted was devastating as the bodies of Bear's crew littered the streets like so many piles of rubbish. He didn't know if Bear was among the dead, but even if he weren't, he would have a hard time recovering from this massacre. Bear had led his men into a death trap, so who would want to follow him again? He patted Jeff on his back and said, "Let's go. We have to meet the others at the warehouse." Jeff seemed as if he was in a trance, staring at the bloody remains of Damion and feeling such a surge of satisfaction that he wanted to go down there and claim his head like a macabre trophy.

"Aight, Shine, now you rest in peace," he whispered. He then followed Blink down the steps and out the building from the rear. The plan had worked perfectly, and they had placed their shooters in positions that guaranteed the most success without suffering any casualties themselves. Sure, they would have to find another stash house and set up another strip to move their product, but it was worth it. Revenge is sweet.

The sniper watched from his vantage point and smiled with satisfaction as he saw Bear's team get decimated. It was a beautiful setup, he grimly thought, and a grudging respect for this guy Blink began to grow. He still had to go because in the end, he was still a drug dealer, but he could admire resourcefulness. His smile stretched even further as he saw Bear and his bodyguard dart from the rear of the building. "So the snake does have more than one skin," he said to himself. This was as it should be because the pleasure of cutting off the snake's head should be his alone. His family was the one who had suffered, so it was only right that the source of their suffering should perish by his hands. Yes, he thought to himself, as he started the engine. He knew exactly where Bear would run to lick his wounds, and he would be there to greet him. Then he'd see to Blink.

As Blink and Jeff entered the warehouse, it was six forty-five, and everybody was already there. They were abuzz with their earlier victory and followed their leaders into the large empty dock area. Many of them recoiled in shock and disbelief as they were greeted by the sight of Moon securely tied and gagged as they knew he was one of the inner circle and a lieutenant in the crew. "Ladies and gentlemen, if I could have your attention for a moment," asked Blink as the crowd's noise began to die down. "I'm sure all of you have questions running through your minds about what's going on and why Moon is in this condition. Well, earlier today, we found out that he had been betraying us. He set up the first raid that got Shiny killed and had made more plans for us to get wiped out today. Finding out about his treachery allowed us to stage the little surprise we had for that crew today, and now I let you decide what his punishment should be." Cries of "death of Judas" and "string him up" filled the air, and Moon's eyes bulged in fear as he was spat upon and repeatedly slapped in the head. "What should it be, people? How do we handle this?"

Shirley stepped to the front of the crowd, brandishing some garden shears. "Let's castrate the bastard. His kind should never be allowed to pass their seed on!" The mass bellowed in agreement and closed in around Moon whose eyes rolled around his head in terror. His chair was flipped on its back, and his pants stripped from his body. Eager hands clutched each leg, and they were pulled into a painful V as Shirley palmed his family jewels and yelled, "This is what traitors have coming here."

"No, Blink, please," he cried. "Don't let them do this to me! Don't, Blink!"

Suddenly he was staring at his own privates in front of his face, blood dripping between Shirley's fingers as she held them high for all to see. Strangely, Moon felt no pain, and as the world swarm around him and he entered the on-rushing darkness that enveloped his mind, his last thought was, *That wasn't too bad.*

\*\*\*\*\*

Detective Lucas Wilson stared down at the mangled corpse lying in the alley among the trash cans and debris. The young man couldn't have been more than twenty-two years old, yet here he lay with his pants gone and his genitals stuffed in his mouth. This was the universal gang sign for a traitor or snitch, but as the body had no ID on it, there would probably be a long delay in notifying next of kin. Hopefully, the prints they got off him would shed some light as to who he was because if he had any kind of arrest record, he would be in the system. The look of terror that was frozen on his face seemed to beckon to Detective Wilson, a man who prided himself on solving the cases that seemed unsolvable. This was getting to be too much for his precinct what with the two mass shootings recently and now this. It was getting as though a person couldn't walk down the street without tripping over a body. He briefly wondered if these cases were connected and decided that he would pursue these cases from that angle. He didn't believe in coincidences, and even though this borough had its share of crimes, this sudden spurt of violence was unprecedented. Maybe there was a new crew trying to take over the territory, or maybe some old beefs were being settled. Either way, he resolved to get to the bottom of it because he was determined that this shit wouldn't happen on his watch. He stood up, motioned for the evidence techs to do their thing, and left. He had some people to question. Maybe he'd talk to his old sidekick, Martin. He kept his ear to the streets and knew people in all walks of life. If only he'd return to work, but we each have our own monsters to slay.

\*\*\*\*\*

Bear couldn't believe his situation. Just hours ago, he was the most powerful drug lord in the city with an army of fierce killers ready to back him up. Now he was in hiding, his most ardent soldiers laid out in the street full of lead. How had this happened? Had that faggot-assed Moon set him up? He would never, in a million years, believe Moon had the heart for something like that, much less the smarts. Now he and Gator, his sole surviving bodyguard, were lying low at one of his stash houses. He couldn't risk the chance of returning to his mansion for fear it was being staked out by Blink's crew trying to finish the job. His calls to the remnants of his soldiers went unanswered. Word traveled fast in the streets, and it was already common knowledge to those in the know that he had foolishly lead his team to destruction. His arrogance hadn't let him consider the possibility that he was being set up. He figured, as top dog, no one had the balls to do it. Now he was groveling in a vermin-filled apartment building, licking his wounds in abject humiliation. He knew the one way he had out of this situation, what he had to do to regain his mojo. And although it was the last direction he wished to go, he didn't have much choice in the matter. Reluctantly, he picked up his phone, punched in some numbers, and waited for the voice to pick up on the other end. The sight of his brother's headless body falling to the street steeled his resolve and smothered his pride as his mind kept replaying it.

On the third ring, a smooth voice picked up with a "Yes, my friend, how can I help you?"

# CHAPTER 6

Vito Zarotti was a boss in his own right. Even though he was the eldest son of one of the founding fathers of the syndicate, Vito had carved out a niche of his own and he carried his own weight. Whereas the old dons frowned upon the dope game, Vito used it to gain wealth, power, and political connections beyond even his old man's wildest dreams. As he sat in the high-backed leather chair in the study of his twenty-three-million-dollar mansion in Long Island, he contemplated the path he was about to take. He didn't want to share his throne with anyone, so his desire to be boss of bosses came with a high price tag. It wasn't about the money; he had more than he could spend in three lifetimes. No, his qualms stemmed more from knowing the lives he had to take. Some of these dons he had known since childhood as they did business with his father, and he called more than one of them uncle. He could remember the gifts they'd always bring when visiting the house, a shiny gold piece or something else just as valuable. But they were standing in the way of progress—his. They looked at drugs as the thing that would bring the organization down, not build it up to become more powerful than ever before.

Meanwhile, all the inferior people like the Columbians, Jamaicans, Mexicans, and even the niggers used them to become if not more powerful then just as powerful as his own people. The old dons were content with the status quo; Vito would lead the syndicate into the next millennium. Even if his own poppa didn't approve, then oh well, he'd have to go too. As the ringing of the phone broke his reverie, he glanced at the caller ID to see that it was Bear calling. Bear was one of his best outlets, purchasing more of his product than any two of his other customers combined.

"Yes, my friend, how can I help you?" he smoothly purred into the receiver.

"Mr. Zarotti, I need to speak to you in person. Something has happened that only your guidance, wisdom, and experience can make right," spoke Bear deferentially. Vito frowned as he never liked to meet with any of his underlings personally. All his business was handled through a third or even a fourth party. The layers of insulation are what made him so successful in this business over the years.

"Would this have anything to do with the fiasco that you were involved in earlier near 125th Street today?" Vito asked.

*Shit, how the hell did he find out about that so fast?* wondered Bear. "Word really does travel fast in the streets," Bear answered. Vito also made it a rule to never get directly involved in the personal and petty beefs of those he sold to, but he also knew he had to protect his interests and investments.

"Don't say anything else over the phone. Meet me at the place in exactly one hour," he responded. He hung up without waiting for a response and stippled his fingers under his chin. *I thought Bear was a major player in this game and that he could handle his own*, he mused to himself. *If I find out that he's weak and clueless, I'm going to have him removed as well and have someone else installed in that position. These nigger pushers are a dime a dozen, so that won't be difficult.* With that, he summoned his ever-present bodyguard Bruno and told him to assemble his driver and a team to accompany him, ready to depart in twenty minutes.

*****

As the sun rose, Blink's eyes snapped open right on cue. He was different in that he never suffered from that groggy state most people found themselves in immediately after waking; he went instantly from sleep to alert. He knew that today would be a busy one as he still had to find a new stash house and distribute all the new product he had gotten from Nut. Then he had to decide where they'd open the strip at because all the old ones were hot due to the recent extra-curricular activity. He swung his feet out of bed and padded toward the bathroom, rubbing the sleep that gathered at the corners of his eyes. A shower would fully revive him, then he would eat and hit the streets.

After finishing up his hastily prepared bacon and eggs and washing it down with a cold glass of orange juice, Blink picked up his cell phone to see who had called. He had fifteen messages from Kimmy and knew instinctively that none of them would be pleasant. He had been so dog-tired when he got home last night that he had just turned his phone off and went to bed. He figured he might as well face the music, so with a deep breath that he released in a long sigh, he leaned against the refrigerator and dialed her number.

"Well, motherfucker, you finally decided to call me back, huh? I guess after you been out all night long running around with one of your hoes you think it's time to come back home to me? You know what? I don't have time for this shit! I'm a queen and I deserve queen status, and if I can't get that, then I want nothing else to do with you!" With that, she broke the connection. Blink stared stupidly at the phone still dangling from his hand, never having the opportunity to get one word in.

"Yeah, I do know what," he said to himself. "Fuck you! Maybe it's' time to end this thing once and for all because with everything that's going on around me, I definitely don't have time for a woman trying to wild me out. Just one less thing I have to worry about." Although he did have love for Kimmy, he wasn't in love with her; her attitude and jealousy had prevented that from happening. He was sorry to see it end on this note because he liked to be on good terms with those he dealt with in every aspect of his life, past or present. Oh well, he shrugged. He shook it off and punched in some numbers. Jeff answered on the first ring with a cheery "My nigga, what's good?"

"I figured you'd be up and about already," said Blink. "You know we got a full day ahead of us. You ready to get this money?"

"I was born ready, B. Give me forty-five minutes and come scoop me up, aight?" responded Jeff.

"Bet. And make sure you brush your teeth because your morning dragon is something fierce," joked Blink.

"Yeah right. Fuck you, nigga. See you in a few," ended Jeff.

As Jeff pulled the covers back to go handle his toiletries, he took a minute to appreciate Keisha's lovely naked form lying next to him. She definitely had the body of a goddess with all the curves in all the right places, and for the past week, they had been growing closer and closer. She now had more of her things at his house than she had at her own, and Jeff didn't mind one bit. He loved coming home to a hotly prepared meal, and his fat ass cousin Tony was surely tickled to death. Jeff knew that is was time to find his own place; he just never really had a need to before. But the woman lying beside him was making him view things in a different light.

"Um, it's cold, baby," she murmured as she stirred in her sleep. "Put the blankets back on me. Where you going so early in the morning?"

"Got to go get this money," Jeff replied. "But I tell you what. Why don't you go house shopping for us today? I'm sure that whatever you pick out will be exactly what I wanted."

With that, Keisha came fully awake with a squeal. "Are you serious, babe?" she cried joyously as she peppered his face with kisses of excitement. "I can go find us a place of our own?"

"Yeah, I'm serious, love," he said, getting a kick out of her excitement. 'We need our own space, somewhere you can decorate with your own touch and taste. Besides, I'm tired of Tony's fat ass eating up everything you cook."

"This is the happiest day of my life," cooed Keisha. "I'm gonna make you so proud of me." In her excitement, she covered his body with her own, and Jeff's manhood started to rise as he gripped the baby-soft flesh of her meaty behind. The kisses became deeper and lingering, and before long, those moans became those of a couple lost in the throes of heated sexual passion—all thought of everything else outside of the body pounding against yours forgotten as you reached for that platform only attained when the partner with you is the perfect one.

*Oh well*, Jeff thought as he plunged into her satiny wetness. *I hope Blink gets caught up in traffic because I'm sure as hell gonna be late.*

*****

51

The sniper had lain in wait in the woods behind Bear's mansion for hours. He had been sure Bear would be headed here to lick his wounds; maybe he'd guessed wrong. There had been no sign of him, only his staff as they scurried about to and fro, tending to their duties. "I should have checked to see if he had any other residences where he lays his head," he said to himself. He had just been so dead set on completing this mission tonight though, so he might be guilty of tunnel vision and didn't consider the many possible variables when dealing with someone of Bear's resources. However, it was a mistake he could correct because he did know where Bear's main stash house was located, and he knew, without a doubt, that sooner or later he would show up there. If not he'd come back and wait no matter how long it took. Like that famous fighter once said, you can run but you can't hide. He had to show his face at one place or the other, and when he did, the sniper planned to be there to blow it off. He picked up his rifle and night vision goggles and left as quietly as he had come.

*****

"It took you long enough to get down those stairs," Blink said to Jeff as he slid into the passenger seat. "I was getting ready to come check on you."

"Naw, man, I had to tighten Keisha up before I left. I've got her going house hunting for us today," Jeff said with a sheepish grin.

"Don't tell me somebody done tamed the tiger," replied Blink as he gave Jeff a playful shove. Secretly, he was happy for his boy because he knew that Jeff had traveled a rough road up till now. He couldn't bring himself to trust another female because of his past relationships, and if he had finally found someone who could break down those barriers, then Blink was all for it. "My nigga, I'm glad for you. I guess now you can tell her to holler at her girl for me because Kimmy and I are through."

"Yeah right. You know how many times you've told me that before?" asked Jeff.

"This ones' for real though, fam," Blink said. "With all that's been happening, I can't stand the extra headaches she's been causing me. It's time to move on."

"Oh yeah, word. Speaking of our recent troubles, I just found out that Bear escaped our little reception. He wasn't listed among the dead according to our people at city morgue," Jeff informed him. "So you know what that means."

"Yeah," Blink mused. "That ain't good. We gonna have to find that bitch and murk him for good or else our troubles ain't never gonna be over, especially since I know that his brother took that ride downtown in the meat wagon. We can expect him to come back hard."

"Exactly what I was thinking," Jeff replied. "I've got our peoples searching high and low and put out a $20,000 reward for anybody who reaches us with the info about where he's hiding."

"Good thinking, my nigga. Let's also get a rundown on his most permanent crib locations as well as his stash houses. He's got to show at one of those places soon."

"Aight, I'm on it," said Jeff. "Now what's our first order of business?"

"We're gonna go pick up Big Shirley and set her up in an apartment at Brooks Manor so we can set up shop. We been sitting on this work for too long, and it's' time to get our product back out there on the strip. I figure we'll use 122nd and Amsterdam. Ain't nobody throwing down over there, so that territory ought to be up for grabs. Any questions? Aight then, let's roll!"

*****

Bear and Gator pulled up to the place, which, in actuality, was a restaurant Vito owned. They served strictly Italian dishes here, and Vito occasionally used it when he had brief meetings. And he expected this one to be brief as well. He already knew what Bear was going to ask for; he just hadn't decided how much he was going to make him pay. After being frisked by the muscle at the front door, the two men were shown to a table where Vito sat flanked by his bodyguards. Bear approached with his hand extended. "Hello, Mr. Zarotti. I'm glad that you were able to see me on such short notice."

Vito ignored the offered handshake and didn't bother to rise or offer Bear a seat. Instead, he picked up his glass of wine, studied the dark red liquid, and slowly sipped from it. "What seems to be the problem, Kenny? Why am I being forced to meet with you like this?"

Bear recognized the snub but could do little about it. "Well, Mr. Zarotti, it's like this. We seem to have run into some problems with a crew over by the Northside Projects. They control some lucrative real estate there, and we've been trying to expand our operations, but they haven't been agreeable."

"So why don't you take your crew and the rest of your team over there and make them disappear?" asked Vito.

"Uh, my team is kinda spread out right now. That's why I'm here to ask you to back me up. Together we can wipe them out and take over the territory for ourselves," stammered Bear. It was in Vito's mind to wipe out Bear along with this renegade crew, but Vito was smart enough to know that since the neighborhood was black, he'd be better off having a black run it.

"You do realize, of course, that the price for my help would be steep and you'd be sorely taxed?"

Bear's desire for revenge overrode all else, so he readily agreed. "Whatever you want, Mr. Zarotti. I'm sure there'll be more than enough for everybody to eat." In truth, Bear was thinking along the same lines as Vito; once he got rid of Blink's crew and regained the respect of his own team, then he'd have a little surprise for Vito himself. "Just help me get rid of these clowns."

"All right, Kenny," said Vito. "I'll call you tomorrow with the details." He stood up, signaling that the meeting was over. After Bear and Gator left, Vito said to Bruno, "Get me Rafael on the phone. He's the perfect man for this situation."

Rafael Ruggerio was a killer's killer. He had performed so many hits for the mob that his nickname became the Bug Man for exterminating so many problems. His given name was Rafaellonaratzi, but he had anglicized it because it was too hard to pronounce. He now headed up his own death squad, a dedicated team of hitters that he could send anywhere in the world to touch those thought to be untouchable, and he had never failed an assignment. After getting the call from Bruno while lying on the blinding white sands of Cancun where he was vacationing, he turned to the stunningly beautiful green-eyed blond beside him and told her to head back to the hotel to pack their belongings. When she pouted about their vacation being cut short, he said, "Don't worry about it. It'll only take me a couple of days to wrap this up, and then we can go anywhere in the world you want." This brought a squeal of delight from her as she knew that this also meant a prolonged world-class shopping spree, so she put a little something extra in her switch as she hurried away to do his bidding.

*****

Detective Wilson knew he'd caught a lucky break. The mutilated corpse was one James "Moon" Johnson, who had a rap sheet as long as his arm. He was known to be a running mate of Harvey "Lil Harve" Williams, presently a guest at Memorial Hospital. What's more, recently deceased gang member Vincent "Shiny" Bidwell was also part of their clique. It seemed like it was open season on these boys, and they were falling one by one. He knew that their ringleader had to be brought in for questioning, and that was one Howard "Blink" Desmond. He had to do it fast because someone had a vendetta against these boys that was leaving too many bodies littering his streets. He grabbed his jacket from the back of his chair and headed over to Memorial.

Harvey didn't know it yet, but he was about to have one more guest.

Blink and Jeff pulled up to the entrance of the Brooks Manor Apartments, and Shirley let out a shriek of appreciation. "You mean you gonna set me up in one of these boxes, Blink? Talk about moving on up! I bet they even have hot and cold running water up in there too! Keep it up! Y'all gonna spoil me," she quipped.

"Yeah, well, Sheri, long as you keep this product straight, it's all yours. You gonna have to hip your cutters to the new spot though and tell them that the same rules apply," said Blink.

"Oh, don't worry. They'll be here soon as I get settled. I got them bitches on speed dial."

"Aight then, let's get cracking."

*****

When he pulled up into the only available parking spot on the street, the sniper was fortunate enough to catch a glimpse of Bear and his bodyguard entering what he knew to be their main stash house. He had already tried two other locations and was about to give up on it for the day when he decided to try one more. As it turns out, the third time really is the charm. From the bulges under their armpits, he could tell that both men were packing heat even though, in his mind, they were useless because they'd never get the chance to use them. Death would come suddenly and silently. The silencer sitting on top of the briefcase guaranteed that. He waited a few more minutes to make sure the pair weren't immediately coming back out, then slipped out of his car, closing the door quietly behind him. He walked casually down the street before crossing over and climbing a fence to go through the backyards of the houses facing the stash house. When he came to the one directly across, he used the briefcase to smash out the window above the rear-facing door, allowing himself access to the inside. He had already noticed the Condemned sign posted on the front door, so he assumed that no one was here even though, as he made his way to the front of the house, he saw all kinds of debris. Used syringes, empty bottles, and discarded condoms told him that this place was often used by the fiends, so he had to stay alert for them. No matter, he was sure that with all the noise they were bound to make, he would hear them long before they caught a glimpse of him.

He unfastened the briefcase and slowly assembled the Mannlicher 7.62—his favorite weapon because although it was light-weight, whatever he hit with it dropped where it stood. He raised the window in the front room barely an inch, just enough for the silencer-equipped barrel to peek out and sighted on the front door of the stash house. Sooner or later, his prey would show up and he would be ready. Little did he suspect that while he was watching the stash house, someone else was watching the watcher.

*****

Rafael had arrived on a flight earlier that morning and gone directly to Vito's villa. Vito had given him the gist of his assignment, the bulk of the info to be gathered from Bear himself. Having been dispatched to the stash house to collect Bear and discuss strategy, Rafael had pulled up in time to see a tall, lean man paying close attention to the same address he'd been given. With the instincts of a wild animal, he knew that something was suspicious about the man, especially when he saw how carefully the man looked around after getting out of his car and the briefcase he carried. Rafael slunk down lower in his seat and watched in his rearview mirror as the man walked down the street, crossed over, and suddenly disappeared behind the houses on the other side. He watched as, a few minutes later, the window in the front of the house directly across slid up, and he smiled to himself. He could barely make out the gun barrel but instantly knew what it was. After all, that's how he would have done it himself. He unscrewed the dome light in his car and slid across to the passenger's side, letting himself noiselessly out. Using the parked cars for cover, he made his way down the street until he was out of the line of sight of anyone in the house. Then he too crossed over, removing the Desert Eagle from its holster and clicking the safety off. He carefully crossed the yards until he came to the house he wanted. Careful not to step in the broken glass that was littered around the back door, he silently pushed it open and entered on cat's feet.

The sniper saw the door across the street open, and his target stepped onto the porch followed by his big bodyguard. The wait hadn't been long, so his body was still perfectly in tune for the kill. He could see Bear clearly as he made the mistake of leaving the porch light on, presenting a perfect silhouette. The first rule for the sniper was that any unintentional movement of the shooter or gun would spoil the shot. A steady hand, an exhaled breath, and the weapon locked in position with a stable surface—that's how a man killed successfully. He sighted through the scope, put the crosshairs right on Bear's forehead, and slipped his finger inside of the trigger guard. He closed one eye, and suddenly everything went black.

*****

Business was booming for Blink and his crew. The new strip quickly became the hub of the drug scene because word of mouth had their new product on the rise and the fiends couldn't get enough of it. It had been three days since they had relocated Shirley and since then they had opened two other stash houses already. Shirley's cutters were definitely the best in the business and got the most out of the least, so Blink had bumped them up another two hundred dollars more per week. There hadn't been any word on Bear's whereabouts, but with the new dollars came new worries, so Blink had stepped up the security anyway. He was chillin' on the steps when his cell phone started singing on his hip. The number was blocked, so he answered with a gruff "Yo, who this?"

"Are you still giving up that bounty for the 411 on Bear?" the voice on the other end asked.

Blink sat up straight as the caller now had his full attention. "That depends on who I'm talking to and if the info is on the one," he said. "But first of all, I don't do no business over the phone, so come to me correct if you're trying to get paid."

"I'll call you back in one hour so we can discuss where we can meet," the voice responded. "Have the money with you." With that, the line went dead as the mysterious caller hung up.

"Hey, Jeff," Blink called across the street to where Jeff stood, putting a couple of their runners on point. "I need to holler at you for a minute." Jeff sauntered over to Blink and asked what was up. Blink ran down the scenario to him about the caller and the info he was supposed to have.

"Aight then, we'll see what peeps has to say when he hits you again. I'll put Benny in charge, and you and I can roll to see what's up."

"Okay," Blink replied. "I know you got my back. In the meantime, why don't we roll over to Memorial and check on Harve? He's got to be getting better by now."

"Bet. I'll be ready in a minute," Jeff replied, heading over to leave Benny some last-minute instructions. Benny's chest puffed up with his newfound responsibilities. He felt like his star was rising within the crew, and he was determined to play his position.

"Aight, boss, I'll go 'head and handle your business. I'mma hold it down out here." Jeff joined Blink, and the pair headed across town.

\*\*\*\*\*

Detective Wilson had been by every day to interview Harvey since the day he had tracked him here, but so far, Harve hadn't awakened from his coma. He had more than one reason for his persistence though. He knew that sooner or later, even if Harvey never woke up, one of his boys would be by here to see him, maybe even the man Blink himself. He knew that he didn't have anything concrete to hold Blink on, but he could question him into bad health and maybe even convince him that it was in his best interest to accept protective custody. As he sat in his squad car by the entrance, drinking a cup of lukewarm coffee and nibbling on a corned beef sandwich, he noticed a Lexus gliding into the parking lot occupied by two men. As they found a parking space and exited the vehicle, he immediately recognized the one in all black with the diamond-encrusted chains hanging from his neck as the man he sought. He waited until they had entered the lobby until he got out to follow them and caught up as they waited at the receptionist's desk.

"Hello, fellas," he said as he flashed his badge and ID. "I have a couple of questions I hope you don't mind answering, and we can do this one of two ways. We can either go to the cafeteria and do this over a cup of coffee like gentlemen or we can go downtown where I'll have you held as material witnesses. The choice is yours."

Jeff immediately scowled and tensed, preparing to go through the detective and out the door. Blink placed a reassuring hand on his shoulder and said, "How can we help you, Officer?"

Detective Wilson led them over to a couple of chairs in the waiting room and asked, "First, who are you here to see?"

"A friend of ours named Harvey Williams. He was injured in a drive-by shooting a couple of days ago," said Blink.

"That was no drive-by and you know it. That was a full-fledged raid, an attempt to wipe out you and your whole crew," said Detective Wilson. "I know you're at war with another team and you're probably preparing a retaliatory hit as we speak. What I want to know is who they are and where they live."

"I'm sorry, Officer, I don't know what crew you're referring to, and I have no idea who would want to shoot Harve. He's as harmless as a fly," Blink replied smoothly.

"Bullshit. I'm here to find out what's going on, and I won't stand for no Wild West shit. You can't take the law into your own hands and seek revenge. If you do, I'm gonna come down on you just like I do everyone else."

"Well, Officer, I'm not sure that you've come down hard on anyone seeing as how you've made no arrests and probably have no suspects. But like I said, I have absolutely no idea who could have done this. I'm only here out of love and support for my friend."

"Yeah right. And what about you?" asked the detective, turning his attention to Jeff.

"I don't know what the fuck you're talking about," growled Jeff. "I only got in town today."

"Sure you did. And I'm Robin Hood. I want you to know that I'm watching you two, and if you try to solve this yourselves, I'm going to bury both of you under the jail. Now get outta my sight."

"It would be our pleasure," said Blink as they stood up and headed to the elevators to see Harve.

*****

DON'T BLINK

Bear stepped out on the porch of the stash house, scanning the street because Vito had called to let him know that someone was coming to see him. When he glanced across the street, he saw someone on the porch over there beckoning to him. As he and Gator headed over, they both kept their hands near their guns, nervous about anything that seemed out of the ordinary. When they got within distance, they heard the man whisper, "Bear."

"Yeah, I'm Bear," he responded. "Who are you?"

"I'm Rafael. Vito sent me to see you."

"Well, what the fuck you doing over there? We stay across the street."

"I need your assistance for a moment," Rafael replied. "There's something that you need to see."

Hesitant at first, Bear gave Gator a look that said, "Anything jumps off blast first, we'll ask questions later," and stepped onto the porch and through the doorway. He frowned as he saw the unconscious form of a gloved figure lying on the floor by the front window, then his eyes widened in shock as he saw the rifle with the night vision scope and silencer on it.

"Anybody you know?" asked Rafael, rolling the man onto his back.

"Naw, man, I ain't never seen this nigger before," gasped Bear. "What the fuck is going on?"

"Well, he certainly had plans for you," Rafael answered. "I saw him mapping out your place and followed him over here. I took him out just as he was lining you up in his sights."

"It must be a hit man Blink and his crew sicced on me. I heard he put some paper out on my head," Bear growled.

"Well, help me get him into the car. We'll take him somewhere where we can get some info out of him. Maybe we can turn this around and use it to our advantage," said Rafael. With that, the three men trussed up the still-sleeping sniper's hands and, after making sure the coast was clear, unceremoniously carried him out to the car, and threw him in the back seat. They got in with him and drove off.

"Hey, my man, before I forget to say it, thanks a lot," said Bear.

"Think nothing of it," replied Rafael. "I've got to protect my investment."

\*\*\*\*\*

When Blink and Jeff entered Harvey's room, they saw him still hooked up to the machines and tubes that were there the first time. Therefore, they both jumped back in surprise when Harve opened his eyes and grinned as they approached the bed. "What the fuck, nigga? I thought you were still sleeping in that coma shit, getting ready to visit the next world!" Jeff exclaimed in astonishment.

"Naw, my dude, you know it'll take more than this to lay me down for the dirt nap," said Harvey, still grinning at their amazement. "I just be lying here playing that role because I know that bitch-assed detective stay up in here waiting for me to wake up. He don't know how much of a wait he got coming." They drew closer to the wounded man, shaking his hand gently for fear of causing more damage.

"How you feel, my nigga? You know it ain't the same out there without you," Blink said.

"Man, I'm sore as all hell, but I can't wait to get up out of here. Benny and Link been coming by here every so often, letting me know what's up. So Moon was rotten, huh? There always was something about that nigger that was off. Hey, but good-looking out with my fam though. Mom's told me how you all been getting at her," Harve said.

"Nigga, that's what we do. You one of us for life, so sure we're gonna look out. Glad to see you're awake though. We getting ready to make some major moves, and we need another soldier by our side," said Jeff. Harve then had a sorrowful look on his face as he glanced out the window.

"That's fucked up about Shiny though. He was true-blue, and I'm gonna miss him."

"Yeah, well, we're not finished getting even for that shit," Blink responded. "We hit them where it hurts, but the head snake got away. We on his ass now though. We're supposed to get the rundown on his location in a few." As if on cue, Blink's phone rang with a blocked number, and he motioned with an index finger, indicating the men should give him a second. "Hello," he barked into the phone, "this is Blink."

"I know who it is," responded the voice on the other end. "I called you. If you're still serious about that info on the person we talked about, meet me at five by the Sixth Street. I'll have on a white sweat suit with a black-and-white Knicks' hat. Make sure you bring the money with you."

"How do I know I'm not being set up?" asked Blink. "You may think you can take my money and run or even try to jack me."

"Never that, man. I know your work. But to prove my intentions, just tell your boy Jeff to ask Keisha about her brother. I'll see you at five."

When Blink rehashed the call to Jeff and what was said, he replied, "Yeah, she does have a brother she told me about. Said he made a living out of knowing other people's business, always selling the info to the highest bidder. This should be legit, but just in case, we'll scope the location out early. Any trouble and we start blasting."

"Aight, we should head on out then. Harve, much love to you, baby. We gonna go handle this and be back at you later," said Blink.

"Damn, I wish I was going with y'all," moaned Harvey. "Just be careful. I can't take any more losses to my fam right now." They dapped him up and headed out the door.

*****

The sniper came to with a start. He tried to rise but realized he had been strapped to a chair with his hands tied behind his back. Bits and pieces began to come back to him as he became more alert. They had caught him slipping. If he hadn't been so focused on putting that round through Bear's skull, he would have heard whoever it was that snuck up behind him and put his lights out. He began to take stock of his surroundings and wondered how long he had been out. Judging from the hunger pangs in his stomach, it had been more than twenty-four hours, but hunger was the least of his problems. He assumed from the vast open space that he was in a warehouse of some kind, and only a single light bulb hanging above him illuminated the darkness. The lump on the back of his head was sizeable and tender, and he wondered if he had suffered a concussion. As he looked around, a voice from out of the darkness startled him because he had assumed that he was alone. "Glad you could join us," Rafael hissed as he approached through the gloom and entered the circle of light. "For a while there, I was afraid that I may have tapped you too hard and you weren't coming back, but here you are. I can imagine that there are a thousand questions swirling through your mind, but they will be answered in due time. Right now, we need you to answer a few questions of our own. As a matter of fact, I'll give you a few minutes because my colleagues should be returning from a little errand soon, and I know they'll be interested in what you have to say. Ah, speaking of the devil. Here they come now."

Right on cue, the door on the right side opened and the sniper recoiled a bit as the face of Bear came into view, followed closely by Gator. Gator carried what looked to be a toolbox with him and sat it down in front of Rafael. "Excellent," Rafael gloated. "Exactly what I needed in case our friend here seems reluctant to answer our questions." He turned to glare at the sniper. "But trust me, answer them you shall or I will show you how far the depths of pain can extend." With that, he opened the box to reveal a shiny row of tools of torture and turned the box so the sniper could see them. "Yes, talk to us you shall."

*****

Detective Wilson had immediately arranged for a team to tail Blink and Jeff as they left the hospital. There were five cars in all, and they communicated by walkie-talkie so one team could pick up as one peeled off to allay any suspicions Blink and Jeff may have about being followed. He took the lead himself, falling behind the men in a Toyota Camry that had seen better days. But since no one gave it a second glance, it fit his needs perfectly. He passed the tail off after seven blocks, making a right on Lexington, when he saw the two detectives in the green Crown Vic fall in line. He would pick it up again in four blocks, being directed by the detectives on the walkie-talkies. It seemed like they were headed to the train station. Suddenly, as he neared Sixth Street, he got the call he had been waiting for.

"Detective Wilson, they have pulled over and stopped by the Sixth Street underpass. They seem to be waiting for someone or something. Hold on, one suspect has gotten out of the car and seems to be checking out the area. Oh yeah, something's about to go down here," the detective in the lead car said. Detective Wilson got out of his car around the corner and, with gun drawn, cautiously edged forward. He scanned the areas of the underpass intensely, searching for anything out of place. He looked on as Jeff came back to the car and got in, apparently satisfied by what he had or hadn't seen. Detective Wilson played a hunch and told his team to fall back and let the scenario play itself out. If Blink and Jeff were waiting for someone, they would wait too.

*****

Robert Lomax was what you'd call a professional snitch. He was, in actuality, a confidential informant, but once he learned how valuable certain information was, he started selling it to the highest bidder. He found it to be a viable way to support his budding drug habit. He had already known who Jeff was because he had copped from his runners a few times, but once he started messing with his sister, Keisha, Robert thought he had an inside track. Once he heard about the reward Jeff and Blink had out for the 411 on Bear's location, he decided to do whatever it took to claim it. As his sister and Jeff visited with mom last week, he took advantage of the fact that Jeff had left his cell phone on the kitchen table. He hurriedly copied Blink's phone number down and left without them knowing it. He already knew where Bear stashed and cut his dope at from visiting the old warehouse over in Thompson Heights to cop from his team also. He just had to make sure that this is where Bear would be hiding out.

Once he saw Bear's bodyguard Gator bringing in the essentials for an extended stay, he knew he had hit pay dirt, and after a few anonymous calls to Blink, he was ready to trade this information for cash. This was how he found himself presently crouched in the shadows under the Sixth Street bridge, nervously watching from his hiding place as Jeff got out of the car to look around. He was just about to make his presence known when he spotted Detective Wilson creeping around the corner with a big-ass gun in his hand. He knew Wilson on sight because he was the cop who recruited him as a snitch! He retreated even farther into the shadows, hoping not to be seen, but not wanting to miss out on his chance to make $20,000. He'd never seen that much money at one time in his life, and he'd do whatever it took to get it. As he hid behind a beam, he dialed Blink's number, which was answered on the first ring.

"Yeah, where you at, nigga? It's already five fifteen, so you way late," Blink shouted into the phone.

"That's because you're being followed," said Robert. "There's at least one detective behind y'all. I don't know if he's alone." Blink glanced up in his rearview mirror just in time to see Detective Wilson duck his head back around the corner of the building. He could also see three cars parked across the street that had at least two people apiece in them, so he figured they'd be cops as well.

"Shit," he said to Jeff. "I bet that bitch been on us since we left the hospital."

"You're probably right. But how we gonna shake him so we can do our business with this nigger on your phone?" Jeff asked.

"I've got an idea," Blink responded. To the voice on the phone, he asked, "Hey, what time does the next train pull out?"

"In about three minutes. Why?"

"'Cause in two minutes, I'mma start my car up. I'm betting that when 5-0 hears my engine kick in, he's gonna go running back to his car to follow. When he does, me and my man gonna jump out of here and beat feet into the station. If we time it right, the train will be pulling out and we'll leave these clowns behind. You good with that?" Blink asked.

"Sounds like a plan. The train is pulling up in here now. I'mma be in the first car waiting for y'all." With that, Robert hung up and made his way down to the platform. Blink and Jeff watched the clock, and thirty seconds later, he started the engine and put the car in drive. Sure enough, he could see Detective Wilson running back across the street in between traffic to jump in his car.

"Now!" Blink hollered, and he quickly snatched the key out as he and Jeff exited the car and raced into the gloomy darkness, heading toward the platform. They made it just as the doors were closing, laughing and high-fiving each other as they caught their breath. Just behind them, they heard a voice say, "I see y'all made it," and a short, stocky fellow rose from the seat to greet them.

Immediately, on guard, Blink asked, "You the guy I been talking to?"

"That'd be me," he replied, holding out his hand in greeting. Blink and Jeff both ignored the offered handshake as they continued to study the man, trying to decide if he could be trusted. As if he was a mind reader, the man spoke up, "Hey, you of all people should be able to trust me, Jeff. After all, you are banging my baby sister." He grinned.

Jeff's eyes widened as recognition dawned on him. "You're Keisha's brother, Robert? I've only seen pictures of you, but I didn't know you were around. I had heard that her brother was a sni—"

"Uh, a paid informant," Robert interrupted. "Yeah, it's true. I make my money that way. But I only inform on people who've done me wrong or rapists or child molesters. I feel like they don't deserve anything else anyway. You ain't got nothing to fear from me. All I want to do is make this money. You did bring it, didn't you?"

"That depends upon the information you've got and how good it is," said Blink. "How do I know you're on the level?"

"I'll tell you what," Robert said. "Instead of just giving you the information, I'll take you to the location. Once you see that I've come correct, then you give me the money and I'll split. I'll leave it up to you to handle your business. I ain't got nothing to do with that even though I don't like Bear anyway."

"Aight, that's how we'll move. We gonna have to get off this train and pick up your wheels anyway," Blink said to Jeff. "You know that by now they're all over mine."

"Yeah, you're right," Jeff replied, still sneering at Robert. "Let's make it happen."

*****

Rafael had never seen anything like it. He had been torturing this man for over twenty-four hours, and yet he still refused to divulge any information. He felt the beginnings of a grudging respect for the man's threshold for pain; many had spilled their guts long before now. Bear and Gator had left over an hour ago, gone to pick up the money from the many stash houses they ran. Rafael was left to his devices along with two of his best men, Vicente and Pablo. Both of them had worked for him for so long that they were used to his cruelly inventive methods, and they too looked on with awe as the man stubbornly kept his secrets. Ironically, the one question the man did answer, he answered truthfully. He did not work for Blink and he was no paid assassin. But the truth was not believed, and he suffered all the more because of it.

"Come now. We can end all this unnecessary torture if you'd just tell us where Blink and his main members live. You tell me and we can bandage you up, get you to a hospital. It's not you we want, just the ones you protect with your silence." Both men knew that this was a lie as each of them were aware that as soon as Rafael got the info he wanted, he'd put a bullet in the man's head. Rafael once again touched the end of the wire strapped around the sniper's genitals to the car battery, and the resulting electrical charge jolted the sniper bolt upright in the chair, bare feet buried in a tub of water. The stench of cooking flesh arose in the air, and wisps of smoke danced up to the ceiling. The sniper's head drooped to his chest as merciful blackness engulfed him. Rafael stood up. He had to report to Vito to let him know the progress he had made and also to inform him of the wisdom in just taking Bear and his man out. He himself could run this lucrative hustle as he was impressed by the amount of cash he saw Bear handling. As soon as this problem with Blink's crew was straightened out, that would be the next item on his agenda.

"You two stay and watch him," Rafael told Vicente and Pablo. "If he comes to before I get back, see if he has anything of interest to say. If not, we'll kill him upon my return and pursue other avenues." With that, he turned and went out the door without a backward glance.

*****

Blink, Jeff, and Robert pulled up in front of a dilapidated church front store down the street from the industrial area Robert had directed them to. Jeff killed the lights and engine and turned to Robert who was in the back seat.

"Okay, so now wassup?" he asked. Robert pointed up the block to an abandoned warehouse that had a sign reading ALLIED FREIGHT across the front.

"That's the building right there," he exclaimed. "I saw Bear's man carrying food and chairs up in there myself, and I know that sometimes Bear uses it to stash his stuff when he has an overflow." Just then, they saw a man exiting the building, looking furtively around before getting into a white Benz and pulling off.

"Who's that?" asked Blink.

"I dunno," Robert replied. "But I've done my part. Can I please have the cash you promised me so I can get out of here?" Blink reached for the money belt he had around his waist.

"I'll tell you what. I'll give you half of it now and half when we come back. We got to make sure that the people inside are the people we're after."

"You mean just the two of you are going up in there? And you want me to wait here until you get back? Are both of you crazy? You don't know how many men are in there and you're likely to get your heads blown off! And then where would that leave me? Out of $10,000 that's where!" Robert cried.

"Your concern is touching. If we don't make it back, you can just have the ride, you faggot. It's worth way more than 10 g's," growled Jeff.

Robert seemed pleased. "Now that's a deal," he beamed happily.

*****

Detective Wilson was fuming. Not only had he been fooled but he'd been done so in front of his whole team. Being made to look like the Keystone Kops was not to his liking nor were the jokes that were going around the station at his expense. He'd had Blink's car towed and impounded and was, at this very moment, on his way to get a search warrant that would allow him to go over every inch of the vehicle. He had also called his CI Robert Lomax several times but had only reached his voice mail. He still hadn't gotten a chance to go by his friend Martin's house yet, but he resolved to do so as soon as he got finished processing Blink's car. If there was just the tiniest thing out of order, he'd have Blink behind bars so fast it'd make his head spin. One way or another, he would make them rue the day they made a fool out of him.

*****

Blink and Jeff crept up to the smoky windows of the warehouse, straining their eyes to get a good look inside. Outside, there was only one vehicle parked, so they knew that somebody was inside. Raising his head an inch, Blink could make out the figure of a man tied to a chair. He seemed to be hooked up to some kind of machine, and on either side of him stood a man, both of them holding automatic weapons and smoking cigarettes. They seemed to be the only two in the warehouse besides their captive and had an air of nonchalance about them. He took a closer look at the man tied to the chair and decided that even though he didn't recognize him, he must be an enemy of Bear's.

*An enemy of my enemy is my friend,* he thought and decided to do what he could.

70

Even though Bear and Gator didn't appear to be around, he thought that he'd still leave them a message.

"Jeff, there's two clowns who appear to be on Bear's team inside. They got another nigga tied to a chair, and he seems pretty beaten-up. I'm gonna creep around to the window on the other side, and when I get in position, I'mma blast the one on the right and you hit the one on the left. Okay?"

"Bet, B. I'll wait for your blast and follow your lead," Jeff replied.

"Aight. In a minute." With that, Blink hugged the outer walls and bent the corner to the other side, watching for alarms or debris on the ground that would alert the men inside. Once he reached the far right-hand side window, he peeked in and had a clear view of the goon on the right. He sighted along the barrel of his .45.

Cal took a deep breath and exhaled it. When he squeezed the trigger, he saw the man's mouth fly open in surprise as the heavy slug struck him right between the eyes, depositing most of his head and brains some twelve feet behind him on the wall. A split second later, he heard Jeff's Desert Eagle clap twice, and the other goon joined the first one on the floor. Blink and Jeff quickly scrambled through the windows, guns sweeping in wide arcs in case there were others that they'd missed. Only when satisfied that they were alone did Blink holster his weapon and approached the man in the chair. Even though his gangsta was unquestioned, Blink recoiled in horror at the shape the man was in. His skin was blistered in so many places that it looked like he was shedding, and his eyes were so swollen that they were mere slits.

His lips were mashed to his face and scattered around his feet were tiny white pieces that could only be his teeth. They had truly done a number on him. As Blink began to unhook him from the apparatus, the man groaned and stirred. "Easy, partna. We're gonna get you outta here and drop you off at a hospital somewhere. Okay?" As the sniper regained some form of consciousness, he tried to focus on his liberator's face. Try as he could, his vision wouldn't clear, but he managed to mumble, "No, no hospital. Please just help me get home." Being from that walk of life, Blink quickly figured out that either the man was wanted or had another reason not to want a hospital because with a hospital came police. Still, he tried once again to convince the man. "My nigga, you're in pretty bad shape, and I'm sure you need medical attention. I'm sure you'd be better off at Memorial or Mercy."

"No, if you can just take me to my house please," he insisted. "I can make it from there."

Jeff had other ideas though. "Man, I say we finish what we came to do. Let's wait here until that nigga Bear comes back and twist his wig back. We can set up an ambush, and he'll never know what hit him."

"Dude here looks like he won't last that long," said Blink. "Plus, we don't know how many guns will be traveling with Bear or if we have the firepower for that. C'mon, help me get him to the car and drop him off. Then we can round up a couple of our people and come back here since now we know where he rests his head and do this shit up proper." Jeff wasn't convinced but decided to agree with Blink. He knew his man had a soft side to him and would go out of his way to help people.

That was one of the things that he loved about him and made him a great boss. The sniper couldn't stand on his own, so the two men got on either side of him with an arm draped around his shoulders and half carried and half walked him outside. As they approached Jeff's car, they could see Robert's eyes get bigger with each step.

"Holy shit, niggas, the fuck did y'all do? Who the hell is that you got with you? Y'all must've really fucked him up," he rambled. They placed the sniper in the back seat with him, and he lolled against the window, having lapsed back into unconsciousness.

"Naw, man, we found him like this in the warehouse. Bear's people must've worked him over something fierce. See if you can wake him up. He wants to go home, so I need his address." Robert began lightly slapping the sniper's face, which had turned toward him and paused. "Damn, his face looks familiar. I know I've seen him somewhere before." The sniper came to long enough to mumble his address to them. Jeff put it in his GPS and pulled away from the curb, not feeling as if this was the right thing to do. However, he'd ride or die with his man, so be it.

*****

Two hours after they left, Bear and Gator parked at the back of his warehouse. Bear was in a particular foul mood because his take was short due to one of his workers skimming off the top. He had had to smoke the fool and he was sure that a couple more had it coming also. Seems like everybody thought they could get away with it since that fiasco with his crew. As soon as he and Rafael took care of Blink, he'd tighten his ship back up, and some heads were gonna roll. As the two of them got out of the car carrying two duffel bags apiece, he noticed the broken glass at the side window of the building, and the hairs on the back of his neck stood up. Pulling his gun and motioning for Gator to do the same, he edged up to the rear entrance. Creeping slowly, eyes straining to see the slightest hint of the threat, he stepped through the door into the holding area. The first thing he noticed was the chair where their captive had sat and the bodies of the guards who lay on either side of it.

Crossing the room, he rolled Vicente over on his back and was greeted by the sight of the hole where the right side of his face had been. Pablo, meanwhile, seemed to be sleeping peacefully until he took note of the two bullet holes in the left side of his chest. He then stood and pulled his cell phone from his pocket and dialed the number Rafael had given him.

"Yo, man," he said when it was answered, "I think you might want to get back over here to the warehouse. Our little pigeon has flown the coop, and someone permanently clipped the wings of the two eagles you left with him."

*****

As Jeff pulled up in front of the address the man had given them, he took note of the modest two-story house nestled in the quiet neighborhood. Trees lined the street on both sides, and there wasn't trash or clutter to be seen anywhere. *Damn*, he thought. *I hope Keisha can find us something like this. I could get used to this pretty quick.* Blink got out and took stock of the neighbors' houses, looking to see if anyone was paying notice to them. Robert was deep in thought, struggling to remember where he had seen this man before. Although his face was in much better shape at the time, he was sure that he knew it and that it was pretty important.

Blink gently prodded the man awake and helped him to get out the back seat to lean against the car as he caught his breath and fought off the wave of nausea threatening to overcome him. "I'm okay now, Howard, just help me up the stairs and I'll take it from there."

Blink's eyebrows shot up in confusion at the use of his government name. "How the hell do you know my name?" he asked in astonishment. "Do I know you?"

"No, but I know you, Howard. Or would you prefer I call you Blink?" Jeff's face began to darken like a thundercloud.

"See? I knew this would lead to some bullshit. We shoulda left this nigga where we found him," he said.

"You've got nothing to fear from me," the man replied. "I mean you no harm. At least not anymore. As a matter of fact, I believe I am indebted to you for your assistance."

"My man, you don't owe me anything except an explanation," Blink said. "How do you know my name?"

"Come inside with me for a minute, and I'll explain everything to you."

"Aight, let me holler at this clown in the whip, and I'll be right back. Jeff, help him inside." Blink motioned for Robert to step out of the car and again reached into his money belt. "Here," he said, thrusting ten g's into his hands. "I guess you earned it because you came correct on the info. You're gonna have to catch a cab back to the set though. I got some shit I need to tie up."

"No problem," Robert gushed as he greedily pocketed the money. He was already envisioning how high he was going to get tonight. "We're not that far from where I'm trying to go, and I definitely got cab fare. Hell, I might even tip tonight."

"Aight. Later," said Blink and followed Jeff into the man's house.

*****

Rafael trembled in anger as he stood staring down at the bodies of his dead men. These were two of his best, and he swore that whoever did this was going to pay. He knew that their former captive must have had help because he was in no shape to have done this himself. "Where is the wallet we took from him?" he asked Bear. Bear walked over to the lone desk in the building and opened the drawer.

"Here it is. He must have forgotten all about it." He placed it in Rafael's outstretched hand who looked inside and extracted the photo ID card inside. The address was clearly listed, and Rafael's burning eyes read it with intensity. "We're going to have a busy night," he told Bear. "Not only does Blink and his crew get it tonight, but when we visit our friend here, everybody who is in the house also dies."

*****

Robert's mind just could not let the man's face go. He kept going over and over it during his cab ride while he mentally counted his money. While waiting at a red light, a police car pulled up beside him, and he hurriedly put the money away, worried that they'd lock him up simply for having such a large sum. The policemen glanced idly over at the cab and, as the light turned green, pulled leisurely off. Something clicked in Robert's mind. "That's it! That's it! Now I know where I saw that motherfucker at. He would be down at the precinct when Detective Wilson would pull me in! Son of a bitch is a cop!" he said to himself.

Immediately his greedy nature made him wonder how he could benefit from this knowledge.

"I bet Bear would pay a pretty penny for this info. Hell, it's what I do, selling knowledge to the highest bidder, so I might as well make this pay. Hey, driver, turn this heap around. We got another stop to make first." He gave him the address to the abandoned warehouse and sat back in the seat with a satisfied smile on his face.

Once they had gotten the man cleaned up a bit and as comfortable as his wounds would allow, Blink and Jeff looked at him expectantly. The sniper gave them the bare bones of his story, leaving out how he had stalked Blink and Jeff with the intent on taking them out. He spoke on how he had trailed Bear to his hideout only to be surprised and captured himself, which brought them up-to-date. His next words were the most troubling of all.

"The man who knocked me out and tortured me is an associate of the Zarotti family. He is their most successful assassin and evidently has teamed up with Bear to wipe you out. So by association, you must anticipate that the Zarottis are onboard with this," he said.

Blink found this revelation disturbing, to say the least. He was familiar with the Zarotti family by reputation and knew that they were organized crime of the highest order. He knew that he didn't have the muscle, guns, or resources to match up with them and wondered what his next move would be. Jeff, true to form, simply said, "Fuck 'em. We can go blast the shit outta them too. They want war, let's bring it to their spaghetti-eating asses." Blink, ever the tactician, knew that such an operation could only have one outcome. He had to come up with a plan that would level the playing field, something that would let them fight fire with fire. He asked the man, "Do you know when they plan on moving on us?"

"Right now they don't know where you moved your operations to or where you rest your head. But it's only a matter of time because they have many people in powerful positions on their payroll."

"Yeah, I know what you mean," said Blink. "Jeff, we're gonna have to lie low for a couple of hours. I have an idea that might work, but it's gonna take a minute for the pieces to fall in place. I have to make a couple a calls, and if all goes well, we'll have this shit over and done with before the morning."

"You know I'm with you, homey. Ride or die!" Jeff replied.

When Robert got out in front of the warehouse that he led Blink and Jeff to, he saw Bear's van parked at the curb behind a gleaming white Benz. He told the cabbie to wait after tossing him a fifty-dollar bill and approached the front door nervously. He knocked, and the door was immediately opened as he was snatched inside by his shirt-front. He found three guns pointed at his head and threw his hands up in surrender.

"Who the fuck are you, and what the hell do you want?" growled Bear.

"Wait a minute, wait a minute," cowed Robert. "I have come to you in good faith. I have a little information you might find useful, and hopefully you'll pay me a little something for it." Bear and Gator slowly put their guns away, but the intimidating Italian fella kept his in his hand as he glowered at him.

"I recognize you," said Bear. "Don't you go to one of my shooting houses?"

"Yeah, I've copped from your people a lot of times," replied Robert, gaining confidence. "Like I said, I have some valuable information for you and was wondering how much it was worth."

"Well, why don't you tell us what it is you know, and we'll decide how valuable it is," Bear responded.

"Well," Robert began, "your people here were killed by Blink and Jeff, and they took your hostage with them. Not only that, but your hostage is secretly some kind of cop. I have seen him at the station many times."

"How have you seen him at the station so many times?" Bear asked suspiciously. "What are you, a cop also or some kinda informant?"

"Naw, naw, man. I work with the cleaning crew that handles that precinct," he lied. "So what is this info worth to you?"

In answer, Rafael lifted his gun and placed four evenly spaced shots into his chest and head, blowing him halfway across the room to lie silently next to Vicente.

"I hate snitches most of all," he said. "I have called my team, and all will be assembled here in a few hours. When they come, we will go to this policeman's address and kill them all." He spun on his heels and disappeared into the inner darkness of the warehouse.

The convoy prepared to leave on their voyage to aid in dealing destruction and death. It consisted of vehicles of different types, all nondescript to attract the least amount of attention as possible since the occupants would all be armed to the teeth. Conversion vans, cargo vans, and station wagons alike prepared for the journey north, each member willing and ready to participate in the coming mayhem. The call for assistance had come about forty-five minutes earlier, and it had taken until now to be fully assembled and briefed as to what the plan would be. Twenty team members in all, four in each one of the five vehicles. Their leader gave them one last pep talk and then climbed into the passenger seat of the first vehicle, a conversion van that didn't look like much on the outside but whose engine purred like a well-fed kitty. With a wave of his arm, he started the progression north toward what outcome he didn't know. All he knew was that his people needed help, and that was enough.

\*\*\*\*\*

Detective Wilson was biting his lip in frustration. The investigators and lab technicians had been over Blink's car with a fine-tooth comb, and everything was in order. Not one speck of paraphernalia to be found, even the title, insurance, and registration were spot-on. It would have been easy to plant the goods in the vehicle, but that wasn't his style. He was a no-nonsense, straight-laced, by-the-book kind of detective, truly believing that honestly was the best policy and that right wins out in the end. Nothing could replace good old-fashioned investigation, so with that in mind, he decided it was time to go pay Martin a visit. As investigators go, he was one of the best, and if there was anything to be found, he would find it. Wilson only hoped Martin was recovered from his personal tragedy because ever since it happened, he had seemed changed—distant, as if only part of him were here on this plane of existence. The rest seemed to be on a mission that only he could fathom. No matter, Martin was his best friend, so he'd see him through his time of crisis as Martin had seen him through his. He hopped in his car and headed through the tunnel, headed to Martin's quiet little neighborhood. First, he had a detour to Memorial to take care of.

\*\*\*\*\*

Blink came back upstairs after making his phone calls to find the man asleep and Jeff on his phone. He could hear snippets of the conversation from Jeff's side and knew that his boy was receiving good news.

"So where is the house you found located at?" Jeff asked into the phone. "Oh yeah? Well, that's wonderful, baby. I can't wait to see it. Now I'll be tied up for the rest of the night handling some business, but I promise you that tomorrow will be all about us. We'll go get our furniture then. Aight, I love you too. Bye."

Jeff got off the phone with an embarrassed grin and said to Blink, "Yeah, that was Keisha. She's found us a two-story colonial in some neighborhood that she said is perfect for us. I'mma go by tomorrow to check it out after we handle our shit tonight."

"Man, I'm happy for you," replied Blink. "You need to slow down and smell the roses while you still can, enjoy some of the fruits of our hard labor. Maybe till I move in next door?"

"You know you can't do that," Jeff grinned. "You move in next door, and you know that pretty soon we'd have the whole hood slinging." The two men cracked up at their good-natured ribbing, forgetting for the moment all the turmoil barreling down toward them.

*****

Detective Wilson returned to the hospital just as the nurses were leaving Harvey's room. He asked the older one about Harvey's status, and she replied brightly, "Oh, he's doing fine. As a matter of fact, he'll probably be released to go home tomorrow."

Detective Wilson had an idea that Harvey was trying to play him for a fool, pretending to be under every time he arrived. This time he obtained one of the surgical masks and a doctor's white gown so that his identity wasn't easily apparent. He eased Harvey's door open and backed into it, pulling an empty tray carrier behind him. Harve was up cursing loudly at ESPN as they gave the results of yesterday's games.

"Yeah, Doc, what you want now? The nurses just left from getting me my meds."

Wilson spun around with fire in his eyes. "I see you're wide awake this time, huh? Since you're feeling so much better, I've got some questions to ask you, and if you don't come up with the answers I'm after, we'll see about where you're getting released to, understand?"

He silently closed the door behind him and approached a stunned Harvey with a menacing grin.

*****

Rafael stood in front of the closed dock, addressing his team. They had arrived about thirty minutes ago and were eager for whatever action their leader had lined up for them. Weapons were being checked and loaded, and an outline for the raid was being laid down.

"This is the night we end this charade," boomed Rafael. "First we take down this detective that is responsible for Vicente's and Pablo's deaths, then we wipe out Blink and his entire so-called crew. Squad one, I want you to assault the home from the rear, approach on my signal.

"Second squad, you will be assigned to cover our avenues of escape, and, squad three, I will lead you myself in a frontal attack. We don't know who or how many will be in the house, so use caution. Regardless, kill anyone you may encounter. Any questions? Okay, let's move out."

With that, the twenty-one men headed toward the waiting vehicles, determined to complete their mission with extreme prejudice.

*****

Detective Wilson left the hospital wondering how much of the info he had gleaned from Harvey could be trusted. There was no way he could check on it until he got back to the station, so he decided that he'd continue his journey to Martin's house. Martin had a computer that he could use, and between the two of them, maybe they could formulate a plan of attack that would work. He pulled out of the parking lot and headed to the tunnel, feeling closer to his quarry than ever before.

*****

Rafael's team first cruised down the street past the house he sought, checking out the easiest point of entry. He noticed that there were an unusual number of station wagon vehicles parked along the curb, so he guessed that this neighborhood consisted of a lot of large families. He took note of the well-worn conversion van parked in the yard of the modest two-story colonial that was the target house. Going around the block, he decided that it was time to make the move, so on the second pass, he had his driver stop in front. The doors opened up in the lead van, and the two behind him and armed men rushed across the sidewalk and onto the lawn, weapons being locked and cocked. Before anyone could reach the front door, heads popped up in the parked station wagons and the doors of the conversion van flew open. Rafael and his team were caught completely off guard. The first man out the van was Nut, Blink's connect from DC, and in his hands was an MP5 with a fifty-round clip. He opened up on the invaders, mowing them down like tenpins. His men followed closely behind him, weapons of all kinds spewing forth a torrent of lead that ripped through flesh and metal alike.

Out of one of the station wagons, Blink fired at the attackers like he was in a video game, his eyes searching for his main adversary, Bear. The big man was nowhere to be seen, but he had plenty of other targets to choose from. Rafael's team returned fire with a vengeance, but they were caught out in the open and bunched together. Jeff seemed particularly possessed, the MAC 10 he gripped growing hot as fire as he poured shot after shot at the Italians, delighting in the way their bodies jerked and danced as he riddled them.

"Thought you'd catch us slipping, huh? Kiss your asses goodbye, mutherfuckas!" he shouted, all the while moving forward.

Rafael couldn't believe what was happening. His men were being decimated in front of his eyes, wiped out by what he considered an inferior force. He had no way of knowing that the call Blink placed earlier was to Nut, calling in on the offer of assistance. Nut had brought nineteen stomp-down soldiers with him, and they were enjoying every second of the mayhem they were causing. There was only one direction open to Rafael, and he took it. Running full tilt, he dove headfirst through the plate glass front window and rolled to his feet behind the couch, still clutching one of the twin 9mm's he carried. Firing a couple of shots out the window, he saw two targets fall with head wounds. The return fire was so intense that he was forced to seek refuge in another area of the house. He began to creep down the stairs.

Meanwhile, Bear and Gator, who happened to be with the first squad, continued to sneak up from the rear of the house. As they reached the far corner, they could see the devastation unfolding before them and were shocked. It was a complete and utter massacre. The men from Rafael's team that were with them immediately entered the firefight to aid their comrades, but Bear felt no particular allegiance to them. He felt that his one and only responsibility was to himself, so he fell to the back as the rest of the men pushed forward.

"Shit," he said to Gator. "These spaghetti benders are being chopped to ribbons. Let's find somewhere to hide." His eyes frantically searched the neighboring houses and garages, seeking and dismissing the immediate options. As he turned to the left, he saw a female standing in an open doorway frozen in terror, her eyes stretched wide and a hand over her mouth as she witnessed death and destruction on a scale she never believed possible. "There's our ticket," Bear said to Gator, and the men rushed forward.

Keisha had spent the day buying drapes and blinds for the house she had just purchased for Jeff and her and was happily applying the first touches when she heard what sounded like the beginning of the next world war. She still had the For Sale sign she had plucked out of the yard in her hand when she opened the door and was greeted by the numbing sight of none other than Jeff spraying lead at a number of men on the lawn two doors down. She would never have believed something like this would occur in what she had pictured as the perfect neighborhood, so far away from the blight of the ghetto she had known all her life. Now she was witnessing her very own man play such a lethal part in the drama. As she stood frozen by what she saw, she became aware of the two dangerous-looking men approaching her with guns drawn and aimed at her head. "Aight, bitch, back up inside and don't make a sound, else you're dead," Bear rasped. Her eyes grew wider as he poked the barrel of his gun into her stomach, forcing her back inside. He shut the door behind him and said, "We're gonna wait this shit out. After it's over, we'll leave, but if you cause us any problems, you're one dead bitch."

Detective Wilson heard the gunfire long before he turned the corner to the street Martin lived on. He pulled his car to the curb and took out his binoculars, scarcely believing what he was seeing. Bodies lay everywhere around Martin's lawn, and damn if that doesn't look like Blink directing and leading the massacre. He had made his streets a war zone despite his warnings to him, and now he was fair game. He put in a call for maximum backup, pulled his service revolver from his shoulder holster, and crept down the street using the cars for cover.

The battle was winding down now, and Rafael's team had had little chance. Being out in the open had decimated them, and those that tried to flee caught hot slugs in the back as they turned to run. Blink had seen the man thought to be their leader dive through the window, so he knew that he was in the house somewhere. Stepping over the dead and dying, he entered the doorway gun first, followed closely by Nut who seemed genuinely elated by the shootout.

"Man, we showed them sauce-making bitches a thing or two, didn't we?" he stage-whispered to Blink.

Blink quieted him with a finger to the lips, indicating with a nod of his head that the danger wasn't over yet. Nut caught the meaning and immediately got back on guard. Cautiously, the two men moved toward the stairs, alert for any movement.

Jeff had made his way around the side of the house followed by two of Nut's crew, firing bullets into the invaders who still showed signs of life.

As they crossed over to the next yard where some had fallen while trying to flee, he suddenly heard a voice cry out, "Jeff, look out," and glanced up to see Bear aiming a Tech 11 directly at him.

With nowhere to run, he braced for the impact of the hot slugs he knew were coming, and suddenly, he saw Bear tumbling through the bay windows onto the lawn below. Through the broken glass, he saw something that his eyes couldn't believe. There was Keisha, his Keisha, standing with the For Sale sign still in a batter's position, having struck Bear in the back of the head with a stunning blow.

As he watched in horror Bear's bodyguard Gator riddled her body from head to toe with pellets from both barrels of his shotgun, spots of red blossomed on her body from the entry and exit wounds like flowers. She dropped dead before she hit the floor.

"No!" Jeff screamed, overcome with grief and rage.

He charged through the window while Gator desperately tried to reload his weapon, fumbling with the shells as he watched death approaching. Jeff fired such a prolonged burst from his MAC 10 that Gator's body couldn't even fall. He was suspended in air as round after round tore through his body, performing a macabre death dance as his body was torn to ribbons.

Blink heard the cry of his right-hand man, and immediately, thoughts of the stranger he'd seen entering the house left his mind. He reversed his steps, followed closely by Nut, rushing outside to be by Jeff's side. As he looked frantically around, trying to locate him, he saw Bear rise from a row of bushes two doors up, aiming his weapon at a target out of Blink's field of vision. He jumped over the fence just in time to glimpse through a broken window Jeff picking up an obviously dead female in his arms, crying hysterically.

As he opened his mouth to shout, "Jeff, watch out," Bear fired a fusillade that ripped through Jeff's back, bullets striking him repeatedly.

Blink screamed, "No!" and he and Nut fired at the same time at Bear's hulking figure. The back of his head disappeared in a red spray of gore and blood and his body somersaulted to land facedown on the lawn. Blink dropped his weapon and raced through the broken window to see Jeff lying faceup, coughing up blood but still holding on to the body of a woman he now recognized as Keisha.

"Who would have thought it?" gasped Jeff, choking on the blood that was now filling his lungs. "Who would have had any idea that the house she brought would be here in this very same hood?" He turned his face toward Blink, his eyes dimming as the light inside of them diminished. "I'm sorry, partner, but I ain't gonna be able to watch your back no more. I got to catch up with Keisha, tell her how sorry I am." With that, he smiled his devil-may-care smile, shuddered once more, then was still, the lights in his eyes gone. Blink gently reached down and closed them, barely whispering, "Go to her, my nigga. I'll see you again on the other side. Meet you at the crossroads." He then stood and crossed back through the window.

In the distance, sirens could be heard approaching fast.

Blink turned to Nut and said, "Man, I owe you a debt I can never repay. Know that you got a friend for life. But you need to get your boys and roll up outta here before the heat comes. I'll be at you in a few days when things calm down."

"Aight. We out. Believe me, though, I'm sorry 'bout your boy. He seemed to be a soldier through and through. What about the last man standing?" Nut asked while nodding toward the house they had seen the Italian entering.

"I'mma handle it. All this shit ends tonight," Blink replied. With that, the two men exchanged hugs, and Nut called to his remaining men. Only four would not be making the trip back with them, so they jumped in their vehicles and disappeared down the street, looking back before they turned the corner to see Blink waving a farewell.

*****

Detective Wilson had crept down the street using every available piece of cover and entered Martin's house gun first. He had to check on the status of his friend and find out what this shit was all about. As he moved toward the stairs, he saw the figure of a lean man hovering outside of what he knew to be Martin's basement door, and he dropped down to silently follow. He had to know where Martin was before he announced himself, and he had no idea who the man ahead of him was. He only prayed that he was in time.

Rafael entered the basement on silent feet, eyes quickly growing accustomed to the lack of light. As he moved into the room, he saw that it was a veritable armory—weapons of all makes and models displayed throughout. Suddenly, the door slammed shut behind him, and he whirled around to look into the face of the man who, hours ago, had been his prisoner. The torture he had undergone was still very much in evidence upon his face, but what captured Rafael's attention was the red button of the detonator he had in his hand. It was attached to what appeared to be at least one hundred pounds of c-4 plastic strapped to his body.

"Yeah, you son of a bitch. So we meet again, only this time on my terms and turf. How much of a man are you now?" Rafael's eyes grew wider still as he desperately searched for a way out of his predicament.

"Hello, my friend. I see that you do indeed have the upper hand. I hope you know that this was only business and not personal and that I never truly meant you any harm."

"Tell that to somebody whose skin you haven't pulled from their body," the sniper said.

"Don't kid yourself. This is definitely personal."

Suddenly, the door banged open again, and there stood Detective Wilson, shocked to see the condition his friend Martin was in and shocked deeper still by the explosives he saw strapped to his body. The sniper shouted, "Lucas, what are you doing here?" In the moment that his attention was diverted from him, Rafael made his move, putting two bullets into Martin's body. Martin still had enough strength and life left to depress the detonator, and suddenly everything was gone.

*****

Blink had been approaching the man's house after reacquiring his weapon. As he neared the corner, he saw a man he recognized as Detective Wilson enter through the doorway, so he faded back the way he had come. He was in the process of crossing into the yard where Bear's body lay when, suddenly, he was lifted off his feet to land twenty yards away on his back, looking up into the sky. He idly wondered if that was a roof he saw up there rushing back to earth, and then all sound came back as he rapidly regained his senses. He staggered to his feet and saw that the man's house was there no more. All that was left was a blackened hole in the earth with bricks and masonry scattered around in a semicircle, the houses on either side severely damaged as well. Luckily, the house in between the man's house and the yard where he was took the brunt of the blast, thereby shielding him and saving his life. He could see the flashing red and blue lights, and he knew that there was nothing else he could do there. He glanced through the window at his dead friend's body once more, looked up at the sky, and silently left.

*****

## Channel 8 News Report
Carol Channing Reporting 5:00 p.m.

"Today was a day of death and destruction here in the Carsonville neighborhood of Long Island where, evidently, a team of terrorists attacked and apparently blew up the home of one of the city's most decorated officers. Detectives Martin Nolan and Lucas Wilson died today foiling what police believed was the beginning of a planned siege of the New York area. Sources report that as many as thirty-two bodies have been found."

*****

## A Week Later

Blink and the rest of the crew—Benny, Byrd, everybody and anybody that could walk—stood on the edge of the ocean, looking out to sea. Even Lil Harve was there, leaning on the crutches that would be part of his rehabilitation for a while. They all stood passing around a few blunts and bottles of Ciroc and Henny, everybody feeling that mellow glow that comes when camaraderie is in the air.

Blink had the bodies of Jeff and Keisha cremated together, and now their ashes lay comingled in the gleaming silver urn that he held aloft for all to see.

"We come together today to honor a soldier, one of us who gave his all to his clique and always stayed true to the struggle. May he know that he will forever be loved and missed, never to be replaced in our lives. We now consign his ashes and those of his woman to the waters of our shore to spend eternity ever at peace."

With eyes shining from tears as they unashamedly ran down his face, Blink emptied the urn into the water, followed by blunts and bottles of Henny. After watching for a minute, the group turned as one and headed home.

*****

Vito Zarotti stood looking out over the rolling hills of the east side of his property. He watched as the nearly naked girls romped in the pristine Olympic-sized pool he had installed, but his mind was a million miles away. He had taken the news of Rafael's death pretty hard because the loss of him and his team had severely weakened his standing in the eyes of the organization. He also knew from his informants that Blink had survived the war and was presently prospering on the east side of the city. Vito placed the blame squarely on the shoulders of Blink for his present situation, not to mention the loss of Bear and the cash his crew brought in. A smoldering, all-consuming hatred burned inside his soul because the worse insult was to be embarrassed in the eyes of his peers.

"Enjoy it now, nigger, for your time is rapidly nearing its end."

He turned from the window and stalked into his plush study. He picked up the phone and asked the operator for an overseas connection, waiting until a voice answered on the other end.

"Hello, papa," said Vito, "I need your help."

THE END

# ABOUT THE AUTHOR

Curtis Jones was born in Hampton, Virginia, the sixth of ten children. After moving with his family to Washington, DC, at an early age, he saw the street life unfolding in front of him—all the movers and shakers who got things done outside the law. Determined to make a better life for his family, his dad once again moved, this time to the suburbs of Maryland, where Curtis continued his education and graduated with honors from high school. He presently resides in Baltimore, Maryland, where he is currently at work in finishing several other novels.

CPSIA information can be obtained
at www.ICGtesting.com
Printed in the USA
BVHW030146231019
561854BV00001B/36/P